The Relationtrip

A Slow Burn Travel Romance

Elana Johnson

feel good fiction

The Relationtrip

by
Elana Johnson

Chapter One
Sloane

My mom once told me that to make a marriage work, one had to compromise. "You don't get everything you want," she'd said.

"Ooh, it has a pool," she says now, as she sits at my bar, her plate of dinner long gone. I've washed all the dishes—pots and pans too—and a certain level of exhaustion invades my bones.

"What are you going to do with a pool in Pittsburgh?" I hang up the dishtowel that hasn't seen this much action in months and turn to face her.

She doesn't so much as glance up from my laptop. The one I need to call my best friend and find out the situation with our trip. He'd texted during my last showing, and my mother ambushed me literally at my car as I'd said good-bye to my clients. If my SUV had been unlocked, she'd have been lurking in the passenger seat.

1

Talking on the drive here. Me cooking something last-minute. More talking. Her going on and on about how the house she's shared with my father for the past twenty-five years is too big now. It feels so empty, she'd said an hour ago. Wistfully.

Other times, she talks about Dad like he's the devil himself. I don't really blame her. I'd had no idea he wasn't happy in his marriage of thirty-three years. I've said very little about Dad since Mom took me to lunch and told me the news.

Some of the things she's said...

I can't go there right now, so I paste a tight smile on my face. "Does it have a gym?"

Mom's been looking at condos and fifty-five-plus communities, which I suppose I can't blame her for. I wouldn't want to do yard work and home improvement or maintenance—things she's literally never had to manage on her own.

"Hm." Mom's eyes glaze over, and I turn, open the fridge, slide my phone off the counter in seemingly one motion. I'm the oldest of three girls, and I'm very good friends with my mother. I don't entertain her nightly—usually—but we talk every day. Most days. I've always liked our close relationship, until this major bump in her life.

I feel thrown back in time five years, and I could say all the things she said to me then. I don't, because I know how harshly words can slice through a person's defenses.

Sometimes those are as see-through as plastic wrap. Though it seems strong and can keep things fresh for longer, it can stick to itself, get twisted, and it's actually very, very easy to poke holes through when already stretched tight.

I know the plastic wrap Mom bears is the stretched-tight kind, so I mind my tongue. I have to get her out of here, and as guilty as that makes me feel, I do have other things to do tonight besides entertain her.

411, I send to Logan. The text flips to *read*, and the tension in my shoulders fades enough to make them finally go down.

"Never mind," Mom says. "It's over by Tree Line."

I turn back to her, Logan's response to me nowhere to be found. "What's over by Tree Lane?"

She doesn't answer, and I'm not sure how much more I can take. "Mom—" I start, a loud, shrill trilling cutting me off.

Praise the heavens.

"Oh." She jumps away from the computer, both hands flying up as if someone has a weapon pointed at her and she needs to show them she doesn't have one.

"That's Murph," I say, doing my best not to grab the computer and flee for my bedroom. "I do need to talk to him about our trip." To my own ears, I sound super sympathetic. My smile feels a bit too wide, but Mom slides from the barstool.

"I should go anyway." She sighs, as if leaving my house

3

—which she's used some choice adjectives for in the past—is the worst possible outcome for her evening.

"Okay," I say. "It was so good to see you, Mom." I leave the call ringing, because a 411-distress call means I need Murph to call me, specifically on the computer, and if I don't answer, to call my cell only two minutes later.

I'm hoping I can kiss-kiss Mom good-bye and be headed to my bedroom by the time he rings my cell.

"Thanks for cooking," Mom says as she pauses at the front door to get her jacket. "The chicken was surprisingly juicy." Her compliments aren't always compliments, but I keep the smile hitched in place. It rides my face as she turns to me, steps into my embrace, and then leaves.

The moment the door closes, I feel like I've crossed the finish line of a marathon. I'd be one of those runners who put everything forth and then stumbles mere steps from that finish line. Tonight, I made it, and I spin back to the kitchen as my phone rings.

I'd managed to escape to my room for ten minutes to change my clothes and ditch my heels before making a gourmet feast for dinner—wherein the chicken *was* juicy and delicious, I'll have everyone know—so I'm able to jog back to the kitchen.

Jog is a generous term. Maybe a bouncy power walk. Whatever. I know when I swipe my phone from the countertop, it's about to go to voicemail and I shouldn't have attempted any sort of bouncing, power walking, or jogging.

"Murph," I say in a pant.

"There you are," he says, as if I've missed a meeting. "Let me guess. The Smithsonians demanded you show them yet another colonial, you haven't eaten since that gross pumpkin seed bar you have synced to a ten a.m. alarm on your phone, and you've just now made it back to your car."

I start grinning at the mention of my clients. Not so much that he heard me huffing and puffing. I tell myself it doesn't matter. He's my best friend, despite the fact that we only see each other once a year—on this upcoming mid-winter tropical retreat.

I laugh, Logan Murphy's deeper chuckles mingling in with mine. My heartbeat thrums in the vein in my neck, and I feel...happy. So, so happy, whenever I talk to Logan.

"First," I say. "I'll have you know I made dinner tonight. For my mother and I." I raise my eyebrows and turn toward the master suite. When I'd bought the house, it didn't have one. I worked with an interior designer, and now I have a fabulous master suite with a settee in my bay window, a walk-in closet any woman would die for, and more European glass than any single woman should ever own.

"Chicken or beef?" Murph asks, not even letting me get to my second point.

"Chicken." My feet meet the luxurious carpet in my bedroom, and I further relax.

"I bet it was so dry," he says.

"Totally," I deadpan. "Secondly, my clients' name is

Smithson. Not Smithsonian." I can't erase the grin from my lips. Murph never gets names right. He gets close, but never dead-on. I grab my hamper of dirty clothes and continue when he doesn't reply. "Third, I still have to prep the paperwork for that closing tomorrow, I haven't started my laundry yet, and I have no idea where my passport is, so please tell me we don't need it."

He pulls in a breath. "You're gonna need it, Sloane."

I figured as much. "I'm starting my laundry. Start the story." We've been traveling together every winter for the past five years. This is our sixth trip together, all of them stemming from that fateful day I showed up at the airport for my honeymoon...alone.

"You're just now starting your laundry?"

"You said you'd keep it tropical." I heave the basket into the laundry room, open the washing machine, and proceed to dump the entire contents of the hamper into the bowl. I don't sort. Who has time to sort their laundry? Not me.

"I did," he says.

"Then I only need swimming suits," I say. "I've got those laid out already."

"Of course you do." He sounds perfectly amused, which makes me smile.

"I still need other things," I say.

"No heels," he says. "No blouses. No skirts."

"Some of my cover-ups are skirts."

"I'll allow it." Murph knows how much I work, and

how hard I put myself together. This trip is all about the opposite of that. I can fall apart. I can do nothing. I can relax and rest and reset for another year.

"So tell me where we're going. And what happened with the resort in the Keys?"

"It flooded," he says. "I went down far too many rabbit holes today, until I finally landed on...Belize!"

"Bless you." I drop the washing machine lid and start the cycle.

"It's great," he says, ignoring my tease. "Tropical rain forests with cenotes, the beach with all the snorkeling you love, and the resort is amazing. No cars. Only golf carts. Very quiet. Upscale."

I frown as I leave my laundry room. "Upscale? How much more is this than that place in Florida?"

"I mean, it's Belize," he says. "Not the US. So it's more. You said you could do more."

"I can." I re-enter my bedroom and head over to the side of the bed where I don't sleep. If I didn't work fifteen-hour days, I might have a little white dog. Or a cat. Nope. A dog for sure.

Murph's barks in the background, and he makes me smile.

"It's not that much more," he says. "I called the airline and got our tickets switched. I booked the resort online. Apparently, Belize is pretty full in late January, thus the need for a more...less cheap place."

"Is it adults-only?" It's not that I don't like children. I

do. In fact, since my thirty-first birthday last spring, I've really felt this urge to get back into the boxing ring. The dating boxing ring. It's like a match out there for me. But I should. Find someone to date, that is. Maybe someone to share my life with. Maybe we could have a couple of kids.

"Yes," Murph says, and I snap back to reality. A scoff works its way free from my throat.

I am never getting married. I don't want to do all the work it takes to find someone who can love me. It's too hard, and I don't think I have all the pieces of my heart back yet anyway.

Just when I think I do, my mom takes me to lunch and says my dad told her he's never really loved her. In thirty-three years.

How does someone live a lie for that long?

In truth, I was simultaneously sad for my mom, furious at my father, and relieved I'm not living in a *five*-year-old marriage that would've ended in the same way. Leon Burgiss didn't love me; that's why he didn't show up on our wedding day.

"It's all set," Murph says. "You like nice things, Sloany, and this is *nice*-nice."

"Thank you," I murmur as I take in my swimwear choices waiting on my bed. "Now, help me with the bathing suit options."

"Put me on video."

I tap to do that, and I aim the phone at the bed. "I've got the classic black one-piece, of course."

"Of course," Murph says, his smile in his voice.

I don't have the opportunity to wear a lot of swimming suits in Pittsburgh, so the fact that I have so many is kind of ridiculous. I reason that I only wear one pair of shoes at a time, but I own many pairs of those too. This is no different.

Plus, I was going to get a hot tub last year. I have the cement pad and everything. Then I realized how much more I needed to do—wiring for the plug, all the pH chemically stuff, and the fact that it snows in Pittsburgh for half the year, I swear.

"That bikini is hot," he says.

"It's not a bikini," I say. I have a fair amount of curves, and I prefer a tankini and some bottoms to the stringed type of swimwear.

"It's clearly two pieces," he argues. "The top is pink, and the bottoms are black."

"It's a sports bra and a pair of panties." The bra-top is cute, though. It has a subtle, cream-colored tropical leaf pattern running through the hot pink. The bottoms are almost shorts to contain my booty, with a thick waistband that makes me look sexy and feminine.

But not hot. I love my body, one-hundred percent, how it is. I simply know how to make her feel and look good at the same time.

"Yeah." He clears his throat and hums in that way Murph has. I can't quite describe it, but he does it when he's thinking about something, when he's not sure what to say, and when he's trying to irritate me. I half-expect him to burst out laughing any second now, but he doesn't.

"There are nine," I say as I move the phone down the line without further comment from my best friend.

"Shocking." I flip the phone around and see his brilliant smile. "I'd expect you to have double digits when it comes to your beach clothes."

"Some of them are two pieces."

"Yeah." His thumb covers the camera, and then he disappears. A blip of disappointment cuts through me, but Murph hates doing video calls on his phone. He's already a little self-conscious about the size of his nose, and the close-up and angle of a phone camera doesn't help.

I don't know what he's talking about. He's rugged, with a square jaw and the perfect amount of scruff no matter what time of day it is. He's got eyes that sparkle like the Atlantic Ocean on a clear, gorgeous day, and just because I'm not dating and will never marry doesn't mean I don't know how devastatingly good-looking Murph is.

"I have at least three cover-ups too," I say as the call switches back to talking only. "Maybe four." I focus on the settee, where no less than half a dozen cover-ups lay, waiting for me to deem some of them Chosen Ones and take them to Belize with me.

I sink onto the bed. "Belize, huh?"

"I've never been," he says. "Dinner with your mom, huh?"

I try not to think about the hour's worth of paperwork

that still needs to be done before I can actually go to sleep. "I'm closing my eyes," I whisper, a game Murph and I have played before. "Paint me a picture, Murph."

He starts to talk about what's happening in Superior, Wisconsin, where he lives. "The snowflakes fall down like angel kisses from heaven, lighting on the ship as it eases into the dock..."

Yes, I fall asleep to the deep, sexy, bass timbre of his voice, my head filled with dreams of my upcoming tropical vacation with my gorgeous-inside-and-out best friend.

Chapter Two
Sloane

I round the corner for the baggage claim in Atlanta, the first four or five carousels to my left, and the remaining ones to my right. I have no idea where my bag will be spit out, but I'm willing to bet Murph does.

I texted him the moment I got service, which admittedly was still a few feet above ground. I knew he'd be here already, as his flight had been scheduled to land an hour before mine. We still have four before our last leg to Belize too.

It's barely lunchtime, but my stomach growls. The biscoff on the plane is never enough. And what's with them only giving out the tiny cans of soda now? My mouth sticks together I'm so parched.

Someone moves, and there's Logan Murphy. All six feet, one inch of him. His blond hair needs a trim, as the ends curl slightly along the back of his neck. He's built like a swimmer, with those big shoulders that can make women's knees weak. Those narrow down his back to his waist, and he's wearing a pair of athletic shorts with his gray tee.

He runs some type of business from a home office in Wisconsin, and he has time to run with his dog every day, make homemade meals, and text me back seemingly at the drop of a hat. Everything about him makes me light up, and this time, instead of shrieking and sprinting toward him, I take another calm moment to drink him in.

Mm, yeah, he's good for a thirsty soul.

Surprised at my non-best-friend thoughts, I give myself a little shake. "You're not getting into the ring with Murph," I mutter. The very idea almost has me giggling. Number one, he's never indicated in the slightest that he's interested in me.

He's dated other women in the five years I've known him. A Lauren once, for a few months. Then someone named Christine. She was a complete disaster according to Murph.

He doesn't ask me about my love life. I don't ask him about his, but he does share if he has someone he's excited about.

Murph is the most genuine man I've ever met. If he's listening to someone, he's interested. If he texts me for my opinion, I know he wants it.

He turns, and the world narrows to only him. And in

the Atlanta airport, that's something. Our eyes lock, and Murph's smile floods his face.

I can't help the little shriek as it flies up my throat, and I grab onto my backpack straps and hurry toward him. Not a jog—learned that lesson a couple of nights ago. Several feet from where he stands at carousel seven—with my bag —I break into a little dance.

He laughs, the sound happy enough and deep enough to fill my whole body with a thrum. I join him, pure joy filling me as I reach him, and he envelops me in his arms. "You made it."

"It was touch and go for a minute there," I say.

Murph holds me like a pro, and I don't want the moment to end. I'm suddenly trying to categorize the thrum in my system. Happy to be reunited with my best friend? The man who literally saved me from taking my honeymoon alone?

Or is this fluttering of wings in my veins built from attraction?

Can't be, I tell myself, but I'm not sure why it can't be. Logan Murphy is devastatingly gorgeous, a fact I note for the second time in as many days as he pulls away from me.

"The Atlanta police wouldn't care if the man in front of you was glinting light into your eyes for hours." His grin pulls very kissable lips back to show his perfectly straight, white teeth. He hasn't shaved in at least a week, and the beard is...hot.

I reach up and cradle his face in one hand. "I didn't throw the Coke can," I say, my own smile feeling fond on my face and in my heart. "Besides, it was a mini." I drop my hand, registering that Murph has gone completely still and silent.

He hums in the very next moment, jerks himself to attention, and pulls my bag forward. "I already got it. The line for the bathroom must've been long."

I take the bag, my eyes suddenly unable to meet his. They're dazzling and blue and glint the way pure sunshine does off open water. "Mm hm." I drop one shoulder out of my backpack strap and let the bag swing down to my suitcase. I unzip the top, reach inside, and look up at Murph through my eyelashes.

"And..." I yank out the box of candy I had to stop and buy. "I got you these!"

His gaze flits over to the box before his laugh fills the baggage claim area again. I shake the box of Milk Duds, as if he can't get them in Wisconsin.

Murph takes them from me, his eyes latching onto mine again. This time, I don't look away. "Thank you, Sloany." He hugs me again, the boxy edges of the candy pressing into my back. He takes a breath like he might say something, but then he doesn't.

He does his hum and steps back. "Should we go get over to the international terminal? Get some lunch over there?"

I nod, my voice lodged somewhere deep in my throat. I'm not even sure why. Something churns between us, but

I honestly have no idea what. I turn and take the first step, Murph falling in beside me, and then the tension flees. Just like that. Gone.

Maybe there's nothing there. Maybe it's just because our relationship is usually through chats, texts, phone calls, and random GIFs. Now we're in the same living, breathing space together, and maybe it'll just take a few minutes to normalize.

"Did you meet your deadline?" I ask as I step outside. A blast of icy wind hits me square in the face. "Wow. Who knew it would be so cold in Atlanta?"

"They're having a storm right now," he says. "International terminal shuttle, over here." His long legs eat up way more distance per step than mine do, but I keep up with him just fine. We join the line to get on, and with more people gathered together, it seems less chilly. "Met the deadline. Emailed everything in last night."

Murph grins at me, and I smile on back. "That's fantastic, Murph."

"You?" he asked. "Closing went through okay yesterday?"

"Done," I say proudly. "My third house this month."

"They're gonna put your picture on a plaque again," he teases.

I smile and shake my head. I did win a recognition award from my real estate agency last year, but it's a big place, and they won't pick me again for a while.

We get herded onto the shuttle like cattle, get bussed

over where we need to go, and go through the whole process of checking in, tagging bags, and going through security again. A big German shepherd works the line, with a stern-looking cop, and I nudge Murph.

"Would Titan be able to do that?"

"Well, he is the best specimen of a dog my vet has ever seen." Murph grins and adds, "I sent you that site with all the excursion options. Did you get it?"

"Yeah," I say, holding up my phone. "As I landed."

"We can look over lunch," he says.

"Or the flight there."

He scoffs, those baby blues dancing a jig. "Right. Please. You'll fall asleep in five seconds on the flight."

"I will not." I hold my head up high as the security officer checks my passport. The machine beeps and I leave Murph to pass the test too.

Once we're all re-shod and re-packed, he says, "Burgers and fries?"

"I've been counting on it." I link my arm through his, and he presses his elbow to his side, cutting a look down at me. I keep my eyes down the wide halls of the airport. "I love this trip we take."

"Me too," he murmurs, and because he never says anything that isn't true, I believe him.

"You can have the window." Murph steps past our row to let me in first.

I duck under the overhead storage, drop my pack, and shimmy my way past the armrests. "You'll have to sit in the middle," I say needlessly. If he'll let me, of course I'm going to take the window. Then I only have to press my body up against his instead of his *and* a stranger's.

"It's fine." Murph eases into his seat with the grace of a ballerina, and I fumble around for a good several minutes, getting out my headphones, making sure I have lip stuff and my water nearby, getting my seatbelt buckled, and everything else I need for the next few hours.

Every cell in my body alights where it touches his, and I wonder if he's as acutely aware of how glued together we are.

We finally take off, and I lean my head back against the rest. A sigh moves through my body, and my cells finally stop vibrating. So it's taken five hours for the tension and attraction to seep out of me. It's fine.

It's *Murph.*

He lifts the armrest between us and murmurs, "Okay?"

"Mm, yeah," I whisper. I have my earbuds in, and music playing, and he's right. I'm going to take a much-needed nap on the flight to Belize.

I lean into his shoulder, and he lifts his arm around me. I've cuddled with him plenty of times—on our first trip together, when we were strangers, we shared a bed in a honeymoon suite.

He's my best friend. He knows me; I know him.

"Mm," I say again. "You smell great."

He does. Like leather and spiced apple cider hooked up and had a bottle of deliciously-scented cologne. I take another big breath of it and settle further, a keen sense of finally being relaxed overcoming me. I drift in and out, and at one point, Murph asks me something I don't answer.

I'm pretty sure he presses his lips to my temple and whispers something my ears hold onto and don't let into my brain to make sense of. It doesn't matter. It's Murph, and he'll tell me later.

Chapter Three
Logan

I have no clue what I'm doing. Holding Sloane Sanders in my arms is lethal—at least for me. I can't be doing this. I have to get away from her.

Where? I glance over to the woman on my other side. She's buttoned and polished to perfection, the way Sloane usually is when she sells houses. I took her professional headshot with my cellphone three years ago on the island of Oahu, and I'm surprised she hasn't updated it yet.

Everything about Sloane surprises me. The fact that she's so soft. So feminine. So funny. So put together.

I write women like her into my romance novels, and they always get their happily-ever-after. Even if their lives are messy on the inside, I craft the perfect man for them, and he provides the one thing they've been missing in their life.

I feel like Sloane is the one thing missing in *my* life,

and I take a deep breath, close my eyes, and tell myself, *You will tell her this year. You will tell her how you really feel about her.*

I've had feelings—real feelings—for her for the last three trips. Two solid years. She hasn't been out on a single date since she was left to walk down the aisle and announce to her family and her was-gonna-be groom's family that he wasn't there.

He'd never showed up at the venue. He called her ten minutes after she was supposed to walk down the aisle to let her know he "just couldn't."

I can. I *can* be the man Sloane needs and wants, if only I could open my mouth and tell her. "Ask her," I murmur.

We live in two different states, but I talk to her every single day. Sometimes I don't hear her voice, but we talk often enough that I can imagine it easily. She wasn't fully awake when she told me I smell great. I know she wasn't. Sloane sometimes says things she isn't fully aware of when she's falling asleep and first waking up.

I know this from our first trip together, where she blubbered at the counter next to me, something about her fiancé not showing up for the wedding.

Then she did something absolutely incredible. She squared her shoulders, tugged her backpack straps tighter, and showed the woman her second ticket. "Can I cash it out? Give it to someone?"

The woman gave her a kind, sympathetic smile. "Everyone here has a ticket to somewhere, sweetheart."

I took a step closer. I didn't. Well, I did, but my flight had been canceled. The ticketing agent I'd been working with had gone to get her manager.

Sloane's agent looked at me, and I'd given her the best smile I could muster. "I don't have a ticket," I said.

Sloane looked at me then, her eyes sliding all the way to the floor and back to my face. She'd cocked her head and that gorgeous hip of hers. "You want to take a trip to Mexico with a stranger?"

I don't remember a lot of details after that. I probably shrugged. And hummed. My sister says I hum instead of clearing my throat. "It's halfway between," Hattie tells me. "Sort of a throat-clear-scoff-hum." She'd shaken her head next. "It's annoying is what it is."

I still do it. I don't even know I'm doing it sometimes. It just happens. No matter what, after answering about twenty-seven questions, showing my driver's license and giving her my phone number and address, Sloane had verified I didn't have any warrants out for my arrest and I probably wouldn't murder her on the Riveria Maya.

We'd taken her honeymoon trip together, and we've been taking a tropical retreat every January since. It's the one shining part of my life I would rearrange anything and everything to do, especially now that I've been fantasizing about telling Sloane how I really feel.

"Not a fantasy," I mutter to myself. "You're going to tell her."

She smells like sugar and mint and cola, and I want to taste all of that on my tongue so badly, my fingers curl into a fist. I glare at the screen playing some lame action movie I've put on to distract myself from the delicious female next to me. I want her in my life more than she is. I want her in my house, in my bed.

So you'll tell her, I promise myself for probably the fiftieth time since I boarded a plane in Minneapolis. Tonight, even.

We'll be arriving in Belize about eight o'clock, and I'm exhausted already. *So tomorrow. I'll tell her tomorrow.*

I have a lot of things to tell her, including what I do for a living. When people ask me, I tell them I run my own business from home. Because I do. I write romance novels and publish them. Some myself, and some for one of the biggest publishers in the world.

I should know how to craft my own HEA, but I'm still working out the details. For now, I'm going to copy Sloane and take a nap. It might be the only thing that saves me from shaking her awake and telling her I've been in love with her for over two years.

Instead, I close my eyes, ignore the blasting of guns in my headphones from the stupid movie, and lean over to kiss her forehead. "I really like you, Sloany," I whisper, and then I let myself relax completely.

* * *

Hours, a shuttle ride, and a trek to a golf cart, then a golf cart ride later, I stand at the check-in desk at Oriandon, the luxury resort where I've booked Sloane and I two rooms. "Logan Murphy," I tell the woman across from me.

The desk has been busy tonight, and the scent of steak and shrimp hangs in the air. My stomach grumbles, because it's been hours since the burger and fries in Atlanta. Sloane has hung back, out of the way, guarding our luggage while I deal with keys, getting maps, directions, and towel coupons.

"ID and credit card," the woman says, and I hand them over. She tappety-taps and clicks, a frown appearing between her eyes. "When did you book this room?"

"Tuesday," I say. "Just barely."

She doesn't look at me at all, and that's not good. I've checked into enough hotels and resorts to know. "Give me a minute, please." She speaks in crisp, perfect English, her accent clearly there but easy to understand.

She walks away before I can protest. What would I say anyway? No? You can't have a minute?

I glance over to Sloane, but she's buried in her phone. I know she wants these tropical retreats to be just that—a retreat from the busyness of her life. I want to call her to my side to reassure myself that everything is fine. Of course we have rooms here. I just booked them on Tuesday.

She looks up, sees me, and immediately grabs her suit-case handle and mine. She tows them to the counter. "What's going on?"

"She went somewhere," I say. "I don't know."

Sloane frowns too, but I'm not going to leap over this chest-high counter to look at the computer. Her stomach growls, and I grin at her. "I'm sure the buffet will still be open."

"If it's not, I'm eating off your arm," she teases.

The first hour or so with her had been filled with some tension and nerves. I know they all came from me. It's getting harder and harder for me to conceal how I feel about her. Even now, I let my hand drop to hers, where I give it a quick squeeze and let go.

"Food and a bed," I say. "That's all we really need, right?"

"And frozen drinks on the beach." She smiles too, and we both look at the pair of women who return to the computer station.

"I'm so sorry," the first says, glancing at the two of us before pointing to the screen. The second woman exam-ines it like if she looks long enough, the secret to world peace or the cure for cancer will snap into place.

She finally looks up. "I'm so sorry," she repeats. "We had a computer malfunction—a glitch—and we've over-booked the resort."

"So do we have rooms?" Sloane asks, putting her elbows up on the counter.

"No," the woman says.

My heart sinks to my feet. I've been up since five-thirty this morning, and I gained an hour flying to Belize. I want food and a bed, and I want them both right now.

I blink. "I booked two days ago. There were plenty of rooms."

"Yes, but it was a glitch." The woman wears sympathetic eyes. "I have one room available. I can give it to you for the same rate as the regular room."

I lean into the counter too. "It's not a regular room?"

"How many beds does it have?" Sloane asked. Outside of that first trip, we've always had our own rooms. I'd paced in mine morning and night last year, trying to work up the courage to tell Sloane I wanted to kiss her instead of just whisper secrets about our mothers together.

Girlfriends do that with each other.

I want her to be a different kind of girlfriend for me.

"One bed," the woman said. "It's a king bed, and there is a large couch and sitting area." Her eyes light up. "The balcony is fabulous. Faces the ocean, and it has a jetted tub."

"On the balcony?" Sloane asks, and dang if she doesn't sound interested.

"Yes," the woman says. "It's one of our luxury...honeymoon suites." She looks between me and Sloane. I look between her and Sloane. Sloane looks only at me, her eyebrows raised.

My heartbeat thunders in my chest, and it feels like a herd of wild horses are stampeding through my veins.

I break her gaze and look at the woman. "For the same cost as one regular room?"

"Yes, sir."

I meet Sloane's eyes and know instantly what she wants. We melt into each other's sides, and as I lift my arm around her once again, I say, "I guess we're going to take our second honeymoon then."

Chapter Four
Sloane

I*t's fine*, my feet say with every step. *It's*. Step. *Fine.* Step.

It's. Step. *Fine.* Step.

The "luxury honeymoon suite" is a short golf cart ride away from the swanky front lobby. A man greets Murph almost before the cart has stopped. "Mister Murphy," he says in a smooth voice. "Welcome to Oriandon." He starts to unload the luggage from the back of the cart. The driver jumps down and helps too, and I collect my backpack and slide from the bench seat of the golf cart.

Murph reaches for me, and I go to his side. We follow the butler up to the third floor and down the hall to the very last room. It sits right in the middle of the resort, and I know the view out that window is going to be fan-tabu-lous-tastic. Too bad it's already dark, and I won't be able to see the water until morning.

I can hear it roaring softly in the distance, and the scent of sand, sunscreen, and surf rides on the air. The butler keys his way into our suite and holds the door. "There's champagne," he says. "Chocolate-covered strawberries are in the fridge."

"Thank you," Murph says. My voice dried up back in the lobby. I wasn't anticipating having to share a room with my best friend.

It's fine, I tell myself. I slept on him practically the whole flight here, and we shared a bed as near-strangers years ago. This will be a walk in the park.

It's practical, I tell myself. Why should we each pay for a room? We know how to share a bed without any hanky panky going on.

I cut a glance at Murph as I squeeze by him and enter the room. He wears an unreadable expression, and I don't have time to study his face. Once we're alone, we'll talk. We'll set some boundaries. Friend-zone boundaries. The problem is, my hopes have lodged somewhere near my heart, and now it's beating things like, *But maybe you could be something more with Murph.*

The room smells like bleach and linen, two of my favorite scents. It means there are no germs. It indicates cleanliness. I sigh as I slip my heavy pack from my shoulders and leave it on the long counter that also houses the TV.

I've gone past the bathroom already, which opened with a set of double doors. If I had my own room, I wouldn't have to close those to shower or use the bathroom. With Murph here, I will. I hate showering with the door closed. It steams up the mirror and makes everything muggy and hot.

The bed is huge, stretching to fill the bulk of the room with puffy white pillows, sheets, and comforters. Murph puts his pack on the left corner of it, and I turn toward the sitting room beyond.

I have to go down a step, and the red Spanish tile stretches from corner to corner in the room. There's a lounge-style couch here, as well as a table and chairs. The wall of windows looms in front of me, and I slide open the door.

The curtains get sucked out with the release of pressure, and I see the built-in couch outside. The jetted tub waits to my right.

"I can fill it for you any time you want," the butler says. "Just let us know."

I nod at him and manage to murmur, "Thank you." I go back inside and tuck my hands into my back pockets while Murph talks to the butler on his way out. The door finally gets closed, and Murph twists the lock.

His head hangs down, his hands still on the knobs and deadbolts, almost like he's praying. Then he straightens and faces me. "So," he says.

"So." I make no move to close the distance between us.

Murph takes slow steps, something urgent blazing in those eyes. My throat narrows as he nears, and I have no idea why. My pulse storms, sending lightning strikes through my body, and all I can think is, *I'm so attracted to him.*

When did I start to feel this electric energy between us? Can he feel it too?

He stops a healthy pace away and folds his arms. "You aren't going to kick me in the middle of the night, are you?"

I blink, so discombobulated in this moment. "I mean —maybe."

He grins, and I realize too late that he's teasing. "I don't really want to sleep on this couch." He nods to the lounger. "But I can."

"It's not even flat." It's curved like something I'll probably lay on tomorrow at the beach. It could definitely fit both of us side-by-side, but I don't want to sleep there either.

"You have those jimmy-legs," he says. "So I won't make you promise."

My fingers itch to start unpacking my bag, but Murph makes no move to do anything like that. His gaze holds mine, and I search his face, desperate to understand what I'm seeing there. I know this man really well, but I can't decipher his non-verbal looks very fast. We spend a ton of time talking on the phone, not face-to-face, and before I can identify much, he walks around to the side of the bed I want to sleep on and sinks to the mattress.

"I'm calling for room service," he says as he lifts the phone receiver.

"Okay." I roll my bag to the end of the bed and heft it up to the mattress. I unpack while he orders a ton of food. I'm not going to complain. I'm starving, and I don't want to hunt down the buffet in the dark any more than he does.

"Good thing I mostly packed swimming suits and cover-ups," I say. "Lots of room for your stuff."

Murph rises from the bed, his footsteps landing on the tile. "Sloane."

"Yeah?" I step back from the closet, where I'd been hanging my long maxi-dress cover-up. He's only a foot from me now, and oh, snappers and cracklers. The energy between us is *hot*, and he has to feel that.

My eyes widen, and his do too.

"Are you upset about the room?" he asks. His pinky finger slides along mine, and his gaze drops to our hands.

My skin bursts into flames where he's touched it, and I croak out, "No. Are you?"

He shakes his head. "Not at all." He looks up at me without moving his head, a boyish hope in his face. *Boyish. Hope.*

I have no idea what's happening, but it feels like time has slowed to zero and is flying by at light speed at the same time. I don't know if I'm coming or going, and I certainly can't come up with anything to say.

"I'm thinking of moving," he says out of the blue.

"Oh," I say. "Okay."

"I work from home as it is," he says. "I can live anywhere." He pulls his hand away from where his fingers have been playing with mine. "I hear there's this really great real estate agent in Pittsburgh who can help me find somewhere great to live." A smile curves that mouth, and oh, he's making my knees weak.

Shock courses through me at the same time. Honestly, I need to sit down. Now. "You want to move to Pittsburgh?" I sit down on the counter and brace my hands next to my hips.

"I mean, who *wants* to move to Pittsburgh?" He laughs lightly, but it dies fairly quickly. He half-scoffs and half-hums and shifts his feet. "I'm just saying, I don't have to live in Superior."

"I thought your parents needed help."

"Yeah," he says. "Yep, with yardwork and stuff. But they can hire someone."

I don't know what to say. He's never mentioned being unhappy in Superior. "Why do you want to leave?"

"Because," he says. "I don't have any friends there." He sits next to me and nudges my shoulder with his. "All my friends are in Pittsburgh." A half-smile accompanies him, and I sigh.

I lean my head against his shoulder. "I would love it if you moved to Pittsburgh."

"Would you?"

"Yeah."

Murph puts his hand on my leg, the heat of it burning

through the denim almost instantly. He pulls his hand back as if he can feel that fire too, and he pushes back to standing in the next moment.

"It's probably a good time for a move," he says with his back to me. "I haven't been out with anyone since Clara, and I think I'm ready to start dating again."

My shoulders tense up. "Really?" My voice comes out so squeaky.

He faces me again. "Yeah, really." He looks down at my suitcase, and with horror, I realize the only things left are underthings. I jolt to a standing position and try to block my bag with my body.

It doesn't matter. He's seen the unmentionables already. His eyes fly to mine. "I'm gonna go get a drink." He lurches toward the door.

"Murph," I say.

"Juan Carlos said we could have anything we wanted." He yanks open the door and won't look directly at me. "Diet Coke? Coke Zero?"

"Sure," I say, and he leaves like he's being chased by the boogieman. I look down at my panties and spanx. A sigh flitters out of my mouth. "Great job, Sloane. Why do you have to unpack the moment you arrive in your room?"

I could've waited until he was asleep, and then ferreted my lace and spandex away in secret. Or drawered it while he was in the shower.

I think of him standing under the rainfall shower head, water dripping down his bare body as he soaps up...

I suddenly have to get out of this room too, but I opt for the balcony and the built-in bench seat there. That way, the ocean can talk to me and help me figure out what to do with my raging feelings for Logan.

Thirty minutes later, she's offered me few solutions. Logan cracks the door and says, "Coke Zero, Sloany. And the food is here." He extends the red can of cola toward me, and I stand to take it.

"Logan," I say as I do. He'd started to turn to go back inside, but he freezes now. "I—I don't want this to be weird between us." I gesture with the can of soda pop, which will explode when I open it if I don't stop. I force it to my side. "This is *us*, Logan. We go on this trip every year, and I don't know what's going on this time, but I..." I don't know how to fill in that silence, and Logan won't. He only says what needs to be said.

"You're my best friend. I can't lose that." I step into his chest, and thankfully, he opens his arms to receive me. "We can sleep in the same bed. It's no big deal. I'll eat your mushrooms, and you'll take my red onions, and we'll be fine. Because this is us."

I pull back and look at him. He nods, his rugged jaw tight. "Yeah." His voice sounds strangled and raw. "This is us."

I nod like this thirty-second conversation has fixed the disaster today has been. "Now, I don't think you should start dating anyone in Superior." I edge past him and go into the blessedly cooler room.

"No?"

"No." I shake my head and take a seat at the table. So much food sits before me, all of it making me smile and my stomach do pirouettes. "Because you're going to move to Pittsburgh, and you'll have to break-up with her anyway."

He chuckles as he pulls out the chair across from me. I can't tell him the real reason he can't start dating. I can't even make sense of it inside my own head. All I keep coming back to is if he starts dating someone, then *we* won't be able to go out.

"I'm going to move to Pittsburgh, huh?" He picks up a homemade tortilla chip and swipes it through the guacamole, also homemade.

I select a fish taco, the orange sauce on it smelling a tad spicy. "You're the one who said it, not me." I take a bite, and yep, there's some heat in that sauce. It's fantastic and tangy against the milder fish and cabbage slaw.

Our banter goes back to normal, which only tells me all the snaps, crackles, and pops of electricity from earlier *were* in fact, one-sided.

Re-resigning myself to the fact that I will not be re-entering the dating ring, I finish my fish taco and look at him. "You know who you should go out with?"

He gives me a blue-blazed look. "Who?" he asks in a deadpan. "And don't say—"

"Lucy," we say together. I glare at him and sit back. "Why won't you go out with Lucy?"

"I've never met her," he says coolly. "And I already

know too much about her. *You're* the one who said whoever she ended up with would need at least a million dollars in the bank just to deal with her hypochondriac tendencies."

"I meant that in the nicest way possible." My assistant *has* taken a lot of sick days, and she always has a very doctorly-sounding reason. Sometimes even a note with a signature I can't read.

"Well, I'm not a millionaire." He flashes me a smile, and we say, "Yet," together too. I reach for a fork and slice off a chunk of the brioche French toast. He's ordered all the things I like best, which only reminds me of how well he knows me. How good of friends we are.

"What about you?" Murph asks just as I stick the sugared and candied bite of breakfast in my mouth. "Are you ever going to dip your toes back into the dating pool?"

I suck in a breath, taking with it an unhealthy dose of powdered sugar—and immediately start coughing. And coughing. And coughing.

Chapter Five
Sloane

"Am I ever going to start dating?" I scoff into the perfectly gentle water as it rains down on me from above. After my near-death experience, Murph and I managed to finish eating, wherein I didn't answer his question.

How did he know I'd been thinking about gloving up again? I shake my head, sending droplets of suds against the tile and glass surrounding me. "He doesn't." We're besties, and if he picked up on any of my...longing vibes, that's why.

"Best friends," I tell myself as I rinse my hair. "You're not going to ruin that." My chest goes concave just thinking about losing him. I can't. I won't. Not even for a chance at forever friendship—with benefits.

"What if it doesn't work out?" I tip my head back and let the water pelt my face. Or I wish it would. It's more like a rainforest water massage. "There's no reason to think it'll work out."

I have so many examples of relationships going bust. My parents, for one. After I'd made the announcement that Leon wouldn't be able to attend his own wedding, after I'd gone on my honeymoon with a stranger, I'd stayed with my mom and dad for two weeks.

Along with my two sisters, they'd been my rock. I'd had no idea my dad didn't love my mom. They had whole conversations just by looking at each other. She can finish his sentences; he knows the exact shade of lipstick to buy for her. Their lives have been intertwined for over three decades, and if they can't make it, no one can.

"There's no use even trying," I say as I rub conditioner into my hair. It's thick and probably won't dry until the flight home, but I had to do something to escape the honeymoon suite. I'm still in it, but the bathroom—the shower, specifically—has always been my safe space. I can talk to the water, it doesn't talk back, and then it goes down the drain, taking my secrets with it.

"You're just lonely." I need some reason for all the sparks, all the bubbling, fizzing chemistry between me and Murph. I haven't felt it until now, until I saw him standing in Atlanta, those broad shoulders and that curling blond hair...

My belly flips as if it's gone into pancake mode, and I grit my teeth. "Stop it." He's a beautiful person. I've known that since the moment I met him, sniffling and red-eyed at the ticket counter at Coastal Airways.

"And not just on the outside," I whisper. My mind goes into overdrive then. If he's so great, why can't I try a real, romantic relationship with him? I already know him. He...does something from home. He has a German shepherd mix named Titan that he runs with every day. He lives in Superior, Wisconsin and has a sister named Hattie, who lives with her husband somewhere in Connecticut.

His parents are still married—happily, I suppose—and he helps them with basic home repairs and yard work. He loves the ocean as much as me, so our tropical escapes in the winter are natural. They make sense.

Why can't we make sense together too?

Exhausted, and not just from the full day of traveling, I finally flip off the water. I dry off and wrap the puffy, white towel around myself. I brought in my pajamas, but the humidity hangs in the air, so I open the door a crack.

"Not dressed," I call. "I just need to air out the bathroom."

Murph doesn't answer, which only piques my curiosity. Perhaps he's sitting outside or went to find something baked and delicious for breakfast. I pray for the last one, as he said he'd seen a grab-and-go option on the list of dining choices here at the resort.

I toe the door open wider and eye the door that leads to the hall. It's about six feet from the bathroom door, and the metal latch that would prevent him—or anyone—from being able to get inside isn't engaged.

Glancing toward the bedroom and sitting room only shows me emptiness, and I reason that I have a towel on. He'll see me in less in my two-piece swimming suits tomorrow. "He's already seen you in less," I mutter, and I dash the six feet to throw the deadbolt and the physical metal bar that will prevent the door from opening more than two inches.

Satisfied, I turn back to the bathroom. I freeze when I come face-to-face with Murph. Logan. I blink and shake my head, trying to figure out why I want to call him Logan when he's always been Murph. Is the nickname too intimate? Not intimate enough? Does it imply BFF status when I want girlfriend status?

Confused, I remain frozen and mute. Murph likewise says nothing. His eyes rake down my towel-clad body to my toes, then rebound to my face. "You have a good conversation with yourself?" His devilish grin makes an appearance.

My blood moves like lava through my veins, burning and singeing everything in its path. I lift my head higher. "I did, thank you."

He chuckles. "You always say you'll talk it out in the shower." He backs up a step and leans against the corner of the wall. "I didn't realize you actually meant you talk to yourself."

Panic grips my stomach, keeping it from flipping again, the traitorous thing. "What did you hear?"

"Garbly-gook," he says. "I wasn't eavesdropping." His smile fades, and he turns around. "I didn't mean to startle you. I heard the lock and thought someone was coming in."

I take the quick steps into the bathroom and completely out of the line of sight of the bedroom. "It was just really steamy in here," I call.

He says something that sounds like, "I bet," but I'm not entirely sure. I quickly turban my hair, swipe on my night moisturizer and my deodorant, and step into my pajamas. I'm covered, but I feel a bit indecent when I return to the main room braless. I'm not exactly small-chested, and I glance down to see one of the buttons on my top gapes between my girls.

I quickly cover it and turn my back as I walk in front of the bed. *Of course* I have to sleep on the side furthest from the bathroom. I can't really blame Murph either, because he let me choose.

I sit down on the mattress, my back to him, and press my eyes closed. Why can't I just have the perfect pair of pajamas? Ones that fit me like a glove and make my best friend fall madly in love with me?

Being at war with oneself really is exhausting, and I sigh as I lay back against the pillows. There are more than before, and I look over to Murph. "They brought the pillows."

"When you'd barely turned the water on." His grin reminds me of home, and I have no idea what that means. I'd like to see it every day after work? "This honeymoon suite has its perks."

I smile too, and the gesture feels easy and settled on my face. Finally. "What other perks have you found?"

He lifts his Diet Pepsi. "Free drinks." He drains the last of it, smacks his lips, and plunks the can down on his nightstand. "So, tomorrow. What do you want to do? Sleep in and relax? Find a late breakfast whenever? Chill on the beach or by the pool? Or should we see if we can jump on an adventure last-minute?"

I look back to the TV, which he's put on a soccer match being narrated in Spanish. "Well, seeing as how my definition of 'outdoorsy' is lathering up in sunscreen and ordering frozen drinks from the comfort of the shade, I think I need twenty-four hour notice of any...adventures." I cut him another grin, and he rewards me with a chuckle.

"I figured," he says.

"We always do Lazy Beach Day the day following Travel Day," I say.

"We do."

We fall into comfortable silence, and it takes me a good half-minute to work up the courage to look over to him. His eyes have closed, and his chest rises and falls in a steady, even rhythm. "Two breaths," I mutter. "Unbelievable." It'll probably take me an hour to wind down and fall asleep with Murph in the bed with me, and he's out already. On top of the comforter, too.

Annoying.

"I'm still awake," he says as if he heard my thoughts out loud. I didn't say them, did I?

"You can fall asleep in two breaths, though," I point out as I slide off the bed. "At least get under the blanket first. Then you can fall asleep whenever you want."

He opens his eyes, and they're still just as vibrant and blue as before. He looks wiped out, and I peel back the covers. "Come on, Murph. I won't even build a pillow wall this time." I flash him a grin, hoping he hears the teasing quality of my voice.

He groans as he gets to his feet. "I didn't fill out a questionnaire either." He pulls back the sheet and blanket on his side of the bed. There are easily ten pillows on the bed now, so I could make that wall between us. I don't want to. "Did you need to see my driver's license? Call my boss?"

"I don't see what good that would do," I quip back at him. "*You're* the boss now." He'd been employed on our first trip, and I had called his boss to make sure I wasn't going to be dismembered over the Pacific. A woman has to be careful these days.

"I give out great character recommendations." He grins and peels off his shirt. I'm struck dumb at all the muscles in his chest and abs and shoulders and chest. Did I mention his abs?

It's apparently sunny more often than I thought in Superior too, because he's sporting a tan in mid-winter.

"Is this okay?" he asks. "I usually just sleep in..." He trails off, his hands on the waistband of his shorts. "You know what? I'm gonna leave the shorts on."

I see the ribbed band of his boxers, my internal question about what kind of underwear he prefers suddenly answered. Why I wanted to know is beyond me.

Murph gets back in bed and turns away from me. The view from the back is just as glorious as from the front, because the man has shoulders any woman would salivate over. *You're not just any woman*, I tell myself sternly. *You're his best friend.*

Then I get in bed and give him my back too. My knees hang over the edge of the mattress, only because I don't trust myself not to curl into him and let him hold me all night long.

The silence presses down on me, suffocating like a wet, hot blanket. I roll onto my back with nary a sound and look up to the ceiling. My lamp is still on. The ceiling fan goes round, round, round.

This is the definition of torture. Silence, in a room with someone you've never had any silence with. At least not the uncomfortable kind.

I roll again, this time to snap off the lamp. We're immediately plunged into darkness, and it takes my eyes several moments to adjust enough to see the crack in the drapes that Murph didn't pull all the way closed. A soft light emanates from the direction of the bathroom too, washing over me from behind.

Where Murph is.

I reach to the floor and pick up an extra pillow, bringing it to my chest and hugging it tightly.

"You can't start dating," I say into the silence. Murph doesn't answer right away, and it's definitely been longer than two breaths.

Maybe he's asleep already. For some reason, my heartbeat falls to my knees and then races back into place.

"If you do, then we won't be able to be friends anymore." It's so much easier to talk in the dark, when no one can see me. When Logan can't see me.

Chapter Six
Logan

My pulse skitters through my body. Not really a beat, and not really a thump. It starts out that way, and then scatters, the way the pellets do in a shotgun.

I'm sure Sloane thinks I'm asleep, but I'm as far from that as a person can get. I shouldn't say anything. So I have no idea why my mouth opens, and my voice asks, "Why wouldn't we be able to be friends?"

Sloane gasps, and the bed on her side moves. I jostle with her, rolling toward her.

It's light enough that my eyes catch on hers.

"You're awake," she whispers.

"So are you." I smile at her, but it dims as fast as it appears. "Why can't we be friends if I start dating again?"

Sloane blinks, a thoughtful expression on her face. Her full lips look amazing naked, just as they do with that pale pink lip gloss she wears. Sometimes she paints on dark red lipstick, and I like that too.

I've spent way too much time thinking about my best friend's lips, that's for dang sure.

With her hair swept off her face, and that soft look in her eyes, I sink lower into the pillow and mattress, relaxing. Everything about Sloane soothes me.

"I asked you a question," I remind her.

"Women don't like other women," she says. I know there's more coming, so I stay silent. She lets out a sigh, her eyes falling closed in a soft blink.

"If you started dating...let's say, Lucy. You'll spend all your free time with her, right? Bowling, burgers, birthday parties with just the two of you."

She paints a nice picture, and I immediately think of April, and what the weather in Pittsburgh will be like then. That's when Sloane's birthday is.

"Yeah," I prompt when she goes mute again.

"So when will you see me?" She shakes her head slightly, her chin barely brushing her own pillow. "You won't. Because it'll make Lucy mad. She'll be jealous. She won't get that we're 'just friends.'" She makes air quotes around the last two words.

"Because men aren't *just friends* with women. And if they are, they're either gay or they're secretly wishing they could sleep with them."

"That is not true," I say, though instant heat floods my

face. I've never been happier it's too dark for her to see the flush creeping down my neck to my chest.

"Lucy will think so." Sloane gives me a *so there* look and closes her eyes.

I watch her shoulders rise, the pillow in front of her chest puffing out with her breath. She exhales it slowly, carefully, in a measured way that tells me she's trying to clear her thoughts.

I know, because she's called me late at night before and told me she just needs someone else in the room with her until she goes to sleep. Sloane is a people-person, and I'm actually surprised she's lived alone as long as she has.

There's a moment here, and I should insert my voice into it. Tell her how I really feel, and that I'm not going to move to Pittsburgh to date Lucy or anyone else Sloane sets me up with.

I'm going to move there so I can be with her.

My voice feels like someone has crushed it in their fist and then shoved it down my throat. It's in a ball, and I can't clear it out.

The silence stretches, but it's not as tight as before. We're breathing together now, and my plan to stop by the front desk every hour until they give me my own room dries up.

I reach out and trail my fingers down her bare arm. Her eyes pop open, surprise registering there before she softens again.

"Are you going to play the app?" I ask.

"I don't have to."

"I don't mind." It's not what I want to say, but my courage has failed me. *Just friends* echoes loudly in my ears, my very soul. My heart beats with the words, and I swallow as I smile at her. She shivers, her bottom lip shaking slightly as she returns the grin.

"There's more blanket if you're cold," I say, pulling it up.

"You don't want it?"

My body is blazing hot, but I keep that to myself and simply shake my head.

Sloane takes the extra blanket, pulling it up and over her shoulders at the same time she eases closer to me.

I shift with her, and the next thing I know, we're cuddled together in the middle of the giant king-sized bed. Ten minutes ago, it had felt too small for the two of us. Now it feels like I have miles on either side of me

"I've missed you," she whispers. "Why are things so weird between us?"

I hold her against my chest, wondering what my pulse beats out against her eardrum. Surely she can feel how erratic it is. It's going to betray me, and I can't make it settle down.

"I don't know," I whisper back, stroking her hair. "But this feels nice. This feels like..." I don't know how to finish, so I tell myself to stay quiet.

I do, and Sloane doesn't prompt me. I close my eyes and breathe in the floral scent of her hair. The powdery, soft scent of her skin. The pure femininity of her drives me to the edge, but I keep my cool and mind my manners.

"This sort of feels like the last night of our first trip together," I murmur. She'd warmed up to me quickly, and I've had people tell me I'm charming and easy-going.

We had to share a bed then too, but there wasn't this chest-to-chest cuddling until the last night.

The night we both shared a lot about ourselves. The night we bonded as BFFs.

The night she'd finally told me the whole story of her and Leon.

That guy. I've never met him, but I'd like to introduce him to my right jab and a few choice words for what he did to literally the smartest, nicest, best person in the whole world.

I pull back on my thoughts, because they're not healthy. Sloane hasn't answered, and I listen to her breathe in and out, in and out, in a steady way. Not a controlled way. A way that indicates to me that she's fallen asleep.

"Two breaths," I whisper with a smile. I press a kiss to her forehead and pull her a titch closer.

"I love holding you like this." My voice barely sounds like my own it's so quiet. I barely hear it myself, and Sloane doesn't stir in my arms.

There's so many things I want to say to her, but not in the dark, when she can't hear me. Not when I'll be whispering them to myself and wake up still pining after my best friend.

I don't know when I'll be able to say the things I need to, but I know they're coming. Soon. Fast. This whispered declaration is only the beginning of the tsunami of confessions I need to make...

Sometime in the next ten days.

"Ready?" I ask her as she drains the last of her pineapple juice.

She nods and plunks the glass on the table. We've just eaten a late breakfast as literally the last two people they let into the crepery before they closed it. The waitress hasn't said anything, but I can feel the daggers coming from her eyes. We've stayed too long.

This place screams opulence, and the waitstaff has been nothing but attentive, asking if we want mimosas or Bloody Marys. Our dishes get whisked away almost before the last bite of bananas Foster has touched my lips.

The floor is polished marble—white—with huge windows from floor to ceiling that overlook a fountain... that overlooks the infinity pool...that extends all the way to the ocean.

The view makes my lungs hitch, and I want to grab my notebook and try to capture the beauty in words. It's impossible I know, but it's literally my job to try to make words paint a picture.

In a place like this, though, with all the blues, turquoise, teals, azures, purples, violets, nothing can describe what an eye can see. Our bodies are just incredible, and I blink, taking in the beauty over and over and over.

Every inch of this resort is immaculate, and we passed people repainting archways on the way here, sweeping the sidewalks, and smiling from golf carts and from behind podiums. They're buttoned and polished, and they know every restaurant and every schedule.

"Logan."

"Yep." I get to my feet and extend my hand to Sloane. She's already dressed for the beach in a fabulous blue, black, and white swimming suit with only one strap. Her cover-up is nearly see-through black fabric that falls to mid-thigh.

I see plenty of leg as she turns and stands, and heat shoots straight up my throat. I put a smile on my face and keep her hand in mine as we walk away from the table.

"I just need to run up to the room and get my beach bag," she says when we get back to the building where our honeymoon suite is.

I look from her to the butler. "I can get you set up outside?" He half turns to continue through the building to the beach beyond it.

The view is simply spectacular from our balcony, and

both Sloane and I had stood there with our coffee cups this morning. The sky is so many shades of blue, I can't categorize them all, and I'm certain I've never seen the sky like this anywhere but here.

"Yeah," Sloane says. "You do that, and get me a drink, and I'll be down in a minute." She puts her hand on my forearm. "Okay, Murph?"

"Sure," I say easily.

Her hand slides away, and I hate how all of my concentration had centered on that tiny point of contact between our bodies. She heads for the elevator, and I follow our butler for today.

"Oh, Sloany?" I call, and she twists back to me. "Mango or strawberry?"

A wicked grin curves that mouth I want to taste so badly. "Surprise me."

I chuckle and give her a thumbs up before going with Jorge. He lays out two towels on two side-by-side loungers. He puts up the shade and sends over a waiter.

"Frozen strawberry banana daiquiri," I say. "And can I get a Diet Pepsi with a lot of ice?" I want to drink, but I don't trust myself not to slur out everything I feel for Sloane in a drunken state.

I won't do that, though I've gotten myself plenty snockered over this woman in Wisconsin. She can never come there and meet anyone, because they all know how I feel about her. Oh, yeah. The key to my vault is definitely whiskey. Or scotch. Or vodka.

I wait about ten minutes before the drinks show up, and I pull out my phone to text Sloane. She should be here by now, and I need the sunscreen she said she had.

I don't have time to thumb out a message before she arrives, out of breath and with the clunk of her bag against the lounger.

"There you are," I say. "Your drink is already here."

She picks it up with a huge grin and takes a long pull on the straw. She smacks her lips like maybe she's already had a little bit to drink, and I raise my eyebrows.

I say nothing as she gets situated beside me, and she doesn't pull out her sunscreen before she extracts a book from her bag.

I stare in horror at it. *Love at Sunset* by L.M. Ryan.

I can't breathe. I'm pretty sure Sloane says something to me, but I can't tear my eyes away from her novel.

Chapter Seven
Sloane

Murph is back to acting like a crazy person. I wave my book back and forth, mirroring my other hand. "Hey."

He blinks rapidly and flinches away from me, a grunt coming from his mouth.

"What was that?" I look at the cover of my book. It's an innocent sunset, with a microscopic couple walking hand-in-hand down the beach, their backs to the reader. "What's wrong with you?"

His face turns the shade of a ripe cherry tomato. "Nothing." He faces the beach again. "Sunscreen?"

"Oh, right." I dig in my bag again and hand him the bottle.

"It's the cream kind?" He gives me a look like he could strangle a puppy, and then flips open the bottle. "I hate this kind. I like the spray better."

"Next time," I say with a hint of acid in my tone. "You can bring the sunscreen."

Murph doesn't look at me as he lotions his legs and feet. Then his abs and chest. As he's perched on the end of the lounger, I have a great view over the top of my book. I wish I could take a discreet picture and post it for the author, because she should write a hero like Murph into her next book.

He's that good-looking. That amazing.

Just like that, my frustration rises again. How is it that I'm immediately back to thinking about him improperly?

I'd stood up on the balcony and watched Jorge set up our loungers. Seeing Murph peel his shirt over his head...

I fan myself again in this moment, and flames lick their way through my fingers when he turns toward me and holds out the tube of sunscreen. "Will you do my back?"

"Mm hm." I've rubbed sunscreen into his skin before. I tell myself this will be no different than the other times we've vacationed in tropical locations and helped each other with hard-to-reach parts of our bodies.

Yeah, I'm a huge liar. This is definitely different, and the moment I touch my lathered-with-sunscreen hands to his shoulder blades, I jump back.

A shock sizzles at the origin of contact, and he looks over his shoulder at me. "Sorry," I say. "Must've had some pent-up energy." That's what my mom always used to say when we'd get a little static shock.

This feels like someone has hooked me to a live wire, and Murph is the source of the electricity.

I manage to rub in the lotion without another incident, and then we swap places. I hold my hair up while he does my neck and shoulders, and I must totally be deep inside a fantasy, because I swear he takes forever to get every inch of my skin covered with sunscreen. He even lifts my single suit strap and goes underneath it, in case it moves a little bit while we're swimming.

I feel like butter left out in the sun by the time he finishes, and the only reason I know he has is because of the soft sigh-hum he makes.

I jolt to attention and take the bottle of lotion from him, dropping it unceremoniously into my beach bag. I'd had it packed before we'd left the room that morning, but if Murph noticed how long it took me to come down, he hasn't commented on it.

"Gonna read?" he asks as I pull my cover-up on again. "Or do you want to swim first?"

We both look out to the ocean. I love her with my whole soul. I love the roar she makes in the distance, but how gentle the waves can rock me closer to shore.

I love the way she never stops moving, because I feel like that inside too. If I stop, maybe something will get stagnant, and I won't know how to fix it. I won't even know it's a problem until it is.

Like with Leon. I hadn't known he didn't love me. On

the surface, all the signs were there that he did. Our engagement was only six months, and we'd been dating for eighteen before that. By some accounts, it would be considered fast, and I'd never once—not one time—seen a sign that he wasn't absolutely genuine in his feelings for me.

Later, after the fake honeymoon with Murph, and after I was able to sit down with Leon like a civilized person, he told me he'd given plenty of signs. I'd simply been too blind to see them.

Even now, after he spelled them out, I don't see what I should've done differently. Rose and Kenna, my younger sisters, say it's not me. It was him.

But still.

I was with him. I should've seen something, right?

"This isn't that hard of a question," Murph says. "Come on. The sunscreen is good right now. Let's swim, and then you can dive into your...romance novel."

"Don't make fun of what I read," I say. "I'm on vacation."

"I would never," he says with a smile that isn't mocking or teasing. "I know you like romance. I do too. Those movies you sent me for Christmas? Loved 'em."

"You're just saying that." I let him help me to my feet like a gentleman, and I'm not upset when he tucks his hand into mine and leads me down the sand toward the water.

"Am I? The one with the dog-walker was really cute. I

actually wanted to hire one and see if I'd get a pretty brunette like in the movie." He gives me that devil-may-care grin and a look out of the corner of his eye.

"So you watched one," I say.

"I watched them all," he says. "We talked about them on New Year's Eve."

"Oh, right." We did. I didn't have a date, and neither did he, so we'd texted every hour from eight to midnight, opening new packages of cookies and counting down to the ball drop at the start of the New Year.

It was all done via phone, but I'm starting to realize that it could be considered a "date" ...and it was fantastic. My favorite cookies were the thin mint Oreos, and Logan had deemed the chewy Chips Ahoy his winner.

We reach the water, and I kick off my sandals. I reach for the hem on my cover-up and pull it up and over my head too. Murph lets out an appreciative whistle, and I put one hand on my hip and push it in hard, cocking out the other one.

I'm wearing a navy blue suit with bright white stars on it, and it's a tankini with a thick waistband that sits over the top of the panties. I love it, because it makes me feel feminine and wishful at the same time. The stars hold mystery and wonder for me, and I love wearing them on my body.

I grin and strike new poses every few seconds, while he laughs and pretends to take pictures with his fingers.

He finally grabs onto me and hauls me into a hug, both of us laughing.

He stumbles in the squishier sand, and I know we're going down before it happens. It doesn't matter. The water is the perfect temperature, and we have a shower only steps away from our loungers where we can rinse off.

"Salty," Murph says as he pulls himself further out into the waves. I go with him, because I have the urge to be in the same space as him.

We find a good spot where we can stand and let the waves push and pull us, body-surfing in the glorious Belize sunshine, that pretty sound of the ocean's voice forming words I can't quite understand.

"Do you think we're weird?" I ask.

Murph moves his hands back and forth in the water, timed with the waves. "What do you mean?"

"Us." I gesture to him as if he doesn't know what the word means. "We take this trip every year, and I don't know... Is it weird?"

"No," he says, his voice quiet but with plenty of power. "Lots of people go on trips with their friends."

"*Girls'* trips," I say. "Or a man trip. Brothers." I don't know why I've brought this up. Maybe because after I fell asleep last night—quickly too, I might add—I'd awakened in the middle of the night to my irrational hour.

Thoughts that plague me after I go to the bathroom and can't fall immediately back to sleep. Last night, all I could think about was me and Murph, and if our relationship is weird.

"We were supposed to have two rooms," I say. "We've always had two rooms. But this time, there's only one, and I slept—we slept—great." I clear my throat, annoyed that the waves buoy him up so I can't see his face.

He's wearing sunglasses anyway, but I know Murph. I can read him the way I read my romance novels.

Usually.

Lately, not so much.

"I said this last night," he says. "I think you were already asleep." He clears his throat too, causing my eyebrows to fly off my face. Murph never clears his throat. He hums. The most I've ever heard is half a clear, and that was followed by a legit cough when he had a sinus infection a few months ago.

I wait for him to continue, but only the water roars at us. Sometimes he does this. He thinks if he waits long enough, I'll let him off the hook.

The water slams into me from behind, and I hadn't even realized I'd turned my back on it. I lurch forward, crashing into Murph as I do.

We both yelp and grunt, and my feet get swept out from underneath me. I scramble to find my footing, and when I do, my right sole comes down on something sharp.

I cry out, and Murph is right there. "You okay?"

I yank my foot up, bending my knee and trying to see through the murky, green-gray water. "Blood."

The sight of my own blood is never good. The world sways, and I say, "Sharks," before making a mad dash for the shore.

Running in water? Do not recommend.

I literally face-plant after two steps, and Murph hauls me to my feet again. "Calm down," he says, plain irritation in his voice.

"I'm bleeding." I look up at him as the water laps at our ankles, and Murph does something most surprising.

He bends and swoops me into his arms. I yelp for a third time in as many minutes, and throw my arms around his shoulders and neck.

"Put me down," I say, desperation building in my throat. I'm way too heavy for him to carry, and I feel every pound on my five-foot-five-inch frame with every step he takes in the soft sand.

"Murph." Tears gather in my eyes. "I'm too heavy."

"Shut up," he says. "You are not." He takes me all the way to the lounger, where I balance on my hands braced behind me and lean back while he lifts my foot to his thigh.

"Yeah," he says. "It's bleeding." He signals to someone, and it better be an emergency room doctor or Batman with Band-aids.

It's not. It's Jorge, and he takes one look at my dripping-blood foot, and hisses. "Yes, this is bad," he says. "I'll be right back."

"Bad?" I ask.

"It's not bad." Murph shakes his head, his joviality returning. He grabs the oversized towel Jorge laid out earlier and presses it to the ball of my foot. "It's fine. Barely a puncture."

"You know what?" I ask as the pain dulls with the pressure. "You shouldn't use words like 'puncture' when someone is bleeding."

He laughs, and that relaxes me. "Fair point," he says. "You're not even going to need a Band-aid."

Sure enough, he's finished doctoring me up before Jorge returns with a bandage. It's pink and has Hello Kitty on it. I take it anyway, thank him profusely, and let Murph tape it over my puncture wound.

That done, I reach for my drink. "Shoot, it's melted."

"I'll get you another one."

"Murph, you don't—"

He's already signaling, and what do I care if I get another frozen daiquiri? They're free. So I let him do it, my brain churning through everything he didn't say out in the surf.

"What did you say last night?" I ask.

He looks lazily over to me, probably half-asleep. "Nothing."

"Murph, that is not true."

He looks out to the water again. "It's hard for me to say."

"Just imagine we're back in the room," I tell him. "It's dark, and you're holding me..."

"I love holding you while you sleep," he says. "Okay? That's what I said." He springs to his feet like he's Tigger and needs to bounce away. Is he seriously going to leave right now?

He takes three long strides away—enough for him to disappear from my sight—while I'm still trying to make sense of what he's said.

He loves holding me...while I sleep?

He loves holding me?

As quickly as he left, he's back. He sits on the end of my lounger like a linebacker, nearly tipping me forward. "Look," he says. "I've been trying and trying to find a good time to talk to you about...things. I have so many things to tell you."

He takes a deep breath and runs his hand through his hair. That's so not fair, and a moment of longing accompanies the surprise still coursing through me.

"I don't know how to say it," he says. "There's never a good time. Or a good way. This is why I write things down."

"Just say it." He won't look at me, and I can't reach him without throwing the lounger off-balance again. "Or write it down. Murph, text it to me."

He turns toward me, and my face lights up at the idea. "Go upstairs to the room, and text it to me."

"Are you serious?"

"Yep."

"I can just tell you—"

"La la la la," I yell over him.

"Mature," he calls through my off-key singing. "Yeah, I'm just gonna go." He doesn't say he'll text me all the things he needs to tell me, but he does grab his phone from his lounger and walk away again, my song still hanging in the air after he's gone.

Chapter Eight
Sloane

I don't get a text from Murph for fifteen minutes. Then I get a flurry of them in quick succession.

I have a lot to tell you, but I'm going to start with the one that's been on my mind the longest.

I don't want to start dating anyone in Superior.

If I move to Pittsburgh, it'll be so I can go out with you.

You, Sloane. I can't stop thinking about you.

I have real feelings for you, and I have for a while now.

My heartbeat spirals and accelerates, and I can't believe what I'm reading. I go over it all again.

"He has real feelings for me."

That's what's different between us. I start typing furiously, but none of the letters land in the right spot. I finally get the simple text right and send it.

For how long?

A little over two years.

I jump to my feet and spin toward the balcony. Logan's not standing on it, and I wish I had wings and could fly up there. I march away from the lounger, then sprint back to get my bag. My mind cannot comprehend this.

"Two *years?*" I ask myself. I glance to the ocean. "*Two* years?" I step up onto the step and toward the huge arched walkway that'll take me to the elevator. Jorge looks over to me. "*Two years*, Jorge."

"Two years, si?" He's obviously confused.

I keep on going, and I punch the up button to call the elevator. "Come on." I tap my foot—legit tap my foot—while my phone chimes again. "Nuh uh." I shake my head. "I'm not answering that!" I yell the words up to the walkway of the second floor.

Our room is on the third floor, and by the time I reach the room, I've received at least six more texts. They could be clients or my assistant, but I don't think they are. I think they're all from Murph, and I can't read them.

I swipe my keycard and wait for the door to do that satisfying clicking. I then push into the room, and Murph spins from where he's standing in the sitting area.

"Two years?" I demand as I hold up my phone.

His jaw tightens. He doesn't shrug. He doesn't explain.

Frantic, I look from him to my phone. There are so many messages, my eyes fritz out, and I can't see. "This makes no sense."

"You asked why things were different between us this year," he says. "This is why."

"And last year?"

"I guess I was better at hiding it."

"Two years?" I swipe through his texts. He's said things like, *I have to tell you something about my job,* and *Don't worry about my parents. They'll be thrilled I'm excited about a woman again.*

I can't make sense of the rest of them.

"Murph." I sink onto the bed, so many conflicting things at play now. I look over to him, feeling like crying.

"You told me to tell you," he says in that authoritative way he has. Even as he speaks, he's soft. But I would never contradict him.

"I—didn't know." I lift my phone and let it flop back to my lap, helpless. "I feel so stupid." A tear splashes my cheek, and Murph moves to sit beside me. Close, but not too close.

Best friend close, not boyfriend close.

"Why do *you* feel stupid? I'm the one with the teenage crush."

I meet his eye. "Is that what this is?"

"No," he says simply.

I nod and study the Spanish-style rug on the floor again. I need a professional organizer to sift through my thoughts. "I don't know, Murph."

"You don't know what?" He reaches over and takes my phone out of my hand. He scoots closer, and I can't help it.

The natural thing to do is lean against his shoulder, hold his hand, and let him comfort me.

I do two of those things and wait for him to do the third. "You don't know what?" he asks again.

"I don't know if we can do this," I whisper.

"Why not?" His voice is equally as quiet.

"What if we...blow it all up?" I straighten and meet his gaze with plenty of panic streaming through me. "You're my best friend. No, you know what? You're my *only* friend. I'm no good with men. What if I mess this all up, and I lose you too?" Tears fall from my eyes, and I wipe them away in a hurry. "This is so stupid."

I get to my feet, but Murph tugs on my hand, refusing to let me go. "Sloane."

With my back to him, I say, "I'm not ready to start dating, Logan. I thought I was, maybe. I was going to ask you about it. But now..." Faced with it—faced with going out with him—I can't do it. I can't be the reason we can't be friends.

"I could be your trial date," he says.

I half-scoff and half-scorn-laugh. "No. I would never do that to you." Can't he see he deserves someone amazing? I may never be ready to date again, and he is. He has been for two years.

I get my hand free and fold my arms as I walk into the sitting area. I don't know what to say, but at least my eyes aren't leaking anymore.

"I don't understand why you give him so much power," he says.

"Who?"

"Leon."

I suck in a breath and turn to face Murph. His face is a carefully arranged mask. "I don't give him any power."

"You do," he says, his eyes glued to mine. "You've given him over seven years of your life, and he's still holding you back, to this day."

"Seven years?"

"You dated and were engaged for two," Murph says, holding up the fingers as if I can't keep track of such big numbers. "And it's been five since he left. Seven years, Sloane. When are you going to tell him enough?"

My fists form at my sides. "You have no idea what I had to endure when I walked down that aisle without my father and without a groom at the altar."

"Yes, I do." He stands and glares at me. "I've been hearing about it for five years. I know every detail. I wiped all these tears already. It's obnoxious that you're still crying them for him."

"They're not for him."

"Then who are they for?"

"Maybe they're just tears." I hate that I sniffle in that moment. Murph and I seem locked in a battle of wills, and I'll tell him what. I am not losing this battle. He has *no idea* what I had to do, the shame I've carried, the way people whispered about me. Even if I've told him a time or two. No one does unless they've had to do it.

"Sloane." He sounds tortured, and I hate that I've done that to him. I should be excited about this new prospect. Me and him dating! Isn't that what I've been thinking about for the past twenty-four hours?

Fantasies are never the same as reality. I know that better than anyone. It's like seeing a really cute picture of Cookie Monster cookies on Pinterest. When you try to make them, they look like the bottom of your shoe after you've stepped in blue raspberry gum.

"I'm standing right here," Murph says. "Right in front of you, and I have been for a long time." He spreads his arms wide. "You don't even see me, and that hurts. It hurts, because I like you. I want to go out with you. Kiss you. Hold your hand, and hold you in bed, and move to Pittsburgh to be with you." His chest heaves a single time. "But you have to stop giving Leon all the power. You have to take control of your life again."

"I am in control of my life."

He does that humming, and it's incredibly annoying. "I'm *right here*," he says again, and then he picks up his wallet like he'll leave. "I'm going to get some chips and guac." He doesn't ask me if I want to come. He knows it's one of my favorite foods, and I stand there and watch him walk away from me for the second time that day. "See you downstairs," he says before he pulls open the door and walks out.

It slams, and I flutter and flinch at the jarring noise of it. The room is instantly too quiet, and I hate that I've let him walk away from me again.

"Murph," I say, and I actually do jog up the single step and toward the door. "Murph!" I pull it open and find him turning toward me.

I have no idea what I'm doing. I have no words forming sentences in my head or my mouth. I simply run to him, and he opens his arms and receives me. He certainly knows how to hold a woman, and I could get really used to this level of tenderness and strength all rolled into one god of a man.

"I see you," I say as I pull out of his arms. "I see you, Murph. I do."

He wears a doubtful expression, his sexy jaw tight, and nods. "Okay." He leans down like he might kiss me, but his mouth goes past mine to the hollow of my neck. He breathes in deeply, and I'm not sure why that's so hot, only that it is. It so is.

"Chips and guac?" he whispers in my ear.

I nod. "Where do we go from here?" I ask, afraid to meet his powerful gaze. Things inside my head have settled a little bit, and while I don't agree that I've given Leon the past five years, I can also see Murph's point.

I've shut all men out of my life. I haven't been on a date—not a single date—with anyone new since that fateful day in November. I haven't joined any dating apps.

I've devoted myself to my work, my clients, and my family. And Murph, of course.

With horror, I realize he's right. I've let Leon dictate the past five years of my life. Even though I didn't know it and would've never given him that power. He's had it anyway.

"I hold your hand," Murph says, lifting it between us. He places a kiss near my knuckles, and sparks shoot up my arm. "We sit on the beach and talk. We go out tonight." A smile ticks up the corners of his mouth. "I'll wear my slacks, and you'll put on those sexy heels I saw in the closet, and it'll be a real date."

"A real date," I echo. I can't believe I'm even considering it. I don't want to punch out Murph's lights. I don't want to dance around him, trying to get a better position. But dating really is like being in the boxing ring, and I'm not really a full-contact-sport type of woman.

"I'll hold you in that bed tonight," he whispers, his voice that deep, throaty vibration that makes my stomach flip again. "And we'll go from there." He clears his throat with that hum and tucks his hand in mine. "Okay?"

I nod, because my tongue turned into a knot when he said he'd hold me in bed tonight. I've always been a touchy-feely type of person, and these past five years of no hugging, no kissing, no hand-holding have left a giant drought in my life. No wonder I've been so cuddly with Murph.

No wonder I'm so attracted to him. No wonder things

have been so strained between us. I'm lonely; he's been hiding and repressing feelings for *years*.

We're *different* than we were last year. *I'm* different.

As we descend to the main level, I can't help thinking that we're on Day One of our vacation, and things are already a whole lot more interesting than they were yesterday. New giddiness prances through me as I think about what the next nine days will bring.

I can only pray it's not a total knockout.

Chapter Nine
Logan

I said maybe one hundred words. Maybe two hundred, but my mouth is so dry, I can't put together another sentence. Sloane is likewise quiet, and I'm not sure I like that. A Quiet Sloane is a Thinking Sloane, and I'm sure she's going over and over—and over—those two hundred words I said.

I know I am.

I can't believe I said them. I can't believe Sloane didn't shoot me down instantly, telling me she's not interested. In fact, the glint I saw in her eye suggested she is.

Is interested in dating me.

"You're thinking too hard," she says.

I look up from my phone, where I've been staring. We've ordered the chips and guac and are waiting for it, and as I glance down to my phone, I see it's black. I have been thinking too hard. "I am?" I ask anyway. I cup my face in my hands. "What makes you think that?"

"You haven't spoken since we—since I came after you."

I'll hold you in that bed tonight.

Why in the world did I say that? Probably because I'm worried that if I take her out tonight in those sexy heels, she'll ask me to sleep on the lounger in the sitting area. It'll feel too intimate to her, and I know Sloane isn't ready for that. I mean, it's taken her five years to even realize she's been giving her ex so much power over her daily decisions.

"I don't know what to say." I look up as the waiter arrives with our food. I'm not even close to hungry, but I don't feel like I can simply return to the same set of loungers and continue our beach day as if nothing has happened.

The whole world is new now. *Our* whole world—how we navigate around each other has been thrown into a new orbit.

She looks at the food, then at me shyly. She's changed already, and a flash of regret strikes me. "Maybe I shouldn't have said anything," I say.

"What? Why not?"

I reach for a chip and scoop up an exorbitant amount of guac. "Because you're looking at me differently."

"I am?" She settles back into her chair and folds her arms. All that does is enunciate her cleavage, and I can admit I look at it for more than a moment before shoving my food in my mouth and meeting her eyes again.

She's glaring now, but I've put so much guac in my mouth, I can barely chew it. Sloane waits, the wind catching the ends of her hair and tossing it around. I swallow and give her attitude right back to her. "Yeah, you are," I say. "Do we need to...I don't know. Break down some boxes? Friendship boxes? Or make some dating rules? Something?"

Sloane scoffs and looks out to the water. We've been seated on the patio of the lunchtime café, and the dull roar of the ocean is easily heard. She could stand and take five steps and be on the sand. She doesn't, but when she brings her attention back to me, she's wearing that contemplative face I've seen before.

"This doesn't have to be hard," I say. "We know a lot about each other already, and we can just expand on that."

"Expand how?"

I sigh and reach for my strawberry smoothie. "I don't know, Sloane. Maybe it's too hard." I had no plans past telling her that I have feelings for her. I didn't allow myself to fantasize too much about how she'd react, other than the doomsday scenarios where she slaps me across the face and tells me I'm the most disgusting man she's ever met.

She picks up a chip and takes a delicate bite of it before adding guac to the remaining piece. "It doesn't have to be hard."

"You're making it hard." I raise my eyebrows to punctuate my point, but she doesn't look at me.

"Not on purpose, Logan."

My heart tears for her a little, which is a totally best-friend thing to do. I turn it into a boyfriend moment by reaching across the table and covering her hand with mine. "I know, Sloane. So tell me what you're thinking about starting to date again."

She turns her hand and laces her fingers through mine.

"Not just me," I say. "Anyone. Let's say this totally hot guy was looking for a new house in Pittsburgh." The writer inside me comes to life, creating this character—based completely on me—in the time it takes me to smile.

"He's blond, which is so your type, and he has a dog, so he needs a fenced yard. A doggy door or the ability to put one in without having to use one of those sliding door inserts is preferred."

"How many bedrooms?" she asks.

"Probably three." I pull my hand back and grab a chip along the way. "Two bathrooms. Nice master suite. He can do some handyman things, and he doesn't mind taking care of a few bushes and trees—but he likes his privacy. He doesn't want a condo or a townhome. He doesn't want a parking lot right outside his front door."

Sloane is fully invested, her blue eyes lit from within. "Does this 'totally hot guy' have any hobbies? Things that he might want to be close to?" She's relaxed now, playing along as she dunks another chip and eats it.

"Yeah," I say. "He likes to run with his dog every now and then. If the yard isn't big enough, he'd love a dog park nearby. Stuff like that. Close to things without being close to things."

"He sounds really demanding."

I almost burst out laughing, but I keep my cool. "What if he asked you out? You show him all these amazing houses, and he's undecided. Hasn't bought anything. Won't commit quite yet. But he's interested. He thinks you're gorgeous, and he wants to take you to dinner. Where would you start with him?"

"It's not the same."

"Why not?"

"Because I know you," she says, and she's probably thinking how big of an idiot I am for giving her a scenario where I come to Pittsburgh and buy a house with her as my realtor. "I've known you for five years. We've seen each other at our best and our worst."

"So we're ahead of the game," I say. "Not behind it."

"It's new ground."

"Mm." I watch her face change, and the humming annoys her too. She's never said as much, but I see it plainly on her face. For some reason, that only makes me want to do it louder next time. "So what do you do when you're trying to navigate new ground?"

"I don't know." She looks away again.

"Yes, you do."

"I don't want to talk about this." She settles her sunglasses into place.

I sense I'm going to lose her. "Whenever I'm navigating something new, I take one step at a time."

She stands, but she still won't look at me. "I'm going to walk for a bit."

"Leave your bag," I say. "I'll take it with me."

After dropping it at my feet, she puts one hand on my shoulder for two beats of time and then leaves. I have no idea what she was trying to say with that touch, but it feels meaningful. I should know.

"Well," I mutter to myself. "Something new to learn about her."

She thinks we know everything about each other, but she's wrong. We know the vacation versions of each other. The people we are when we're not getting up in the morning and going to work all day. She has no idea if I wash my dishes immediately after breakfast, or if I leave my socks all over the floor for someone else to pick up later.

She only knows the best parts of me, because those are the only things I've let her see. I quickly wake my phone and text her.

We have so much to learn about each other, I say. I don't know what your daily routine is like. I don't know what you need after a hard day, or what to do to celebrate little things with you. I don't know what your favorite restaurant is, and I could probably guess, but I don't know if you leave your clothes in the dryer for days before folding them, or if you take them out and fold them immediately.

I send that mongo paragraph, and I keep typing. *I know Vacation Sloane. The woman who doesn't work, doesn't prep docs at night, doesn't have to procure her own meals, who basically isn't anything like the Pittsburgh Sloane.*

I swallow, because I'm dangerously close to my next secret. *You know Vacation Logan. Or Fun Guy Murph. You have no idea what I even do all day long, and I bet you can't tell me which cut of steak I'd pick every time.*

Fine, she sends before I get off the last paragraph. I tap *send* and sit back.

You're right, she says. A few seconds later, I get another text from her. *T-bone?*

I grin and can't stop. *T-bone? Really? Is that your final answer?*

Not with that snarky really *thrown in there.*

I chuckle to myself, and this is why I like Sloane so much. Texts like these. I pick up another chip and scoop up some guac. She just needs some time to get a visual of what the next nine days and nights will be like, and then she'll be okay.

I don't need a visual. I don't need plans. Where Sloane likes her routines and her schedules, I don't like to commit to something further than two hours out, because what if I don't want to do it? What if something more interesting is going on?

After finishing the chips and guac, I stand and nearly trip over her beach bag. I pick it up, that romance novel sitting right on top. I pluck it out and hold it in my hand. It's wild seeing my book out in the world. Every single time, it's really weird.

I flip it over and look at the back. Of course there's no author photo, because no one knows L.M. Ryan is me. Well, a few people do. My literary agent, my editor, and the team at my publisher. My sister knows too. That's it. Not even my mother knows.

The pages ruffle in the breeze, and I stuff the book back in Sloane's bag. I'll have to ask her what she likes about it later. Women like her keep me employed, and I can consider it market research.

More than one situation from Sloane's life has made its way into my books, because it's hard to come up with plot points for someone who never leaves the house. She interacts with a lot of people, and boy, does she have some stories to tell.

"You're out there, Belinda," I say to the book cover. My female main character from that book had been hard for me to develop and write, but I'd done it. This is actually one of my self-published titles, which makes it even more exciting to see Sloane reading it in Belize.

I'm going to have to tell her what I do for a living sooner or later, and now that the truth about my crush is out, I have to decide what's most important for her to know next.

"Maybe just take one step at a time," I tell myself, and I shoulder her bag and do exactly that—toward the concierge who can help me book excursions and dinner reservations here at the resort. Sloane and I are going to need something to do for the next nine days, and I'm not spending them having difficult conversations where she walks away and leaves her bag for me to carry back to the room.

Chapter Ten
Sloane

I exit the bathroom and find Logan reading in the sitting area. I can only see the top of his head and his bare feet, but the glow from his eReader makes a halo around his person.

"Done," I say.

He doesn't respond, and I wonder if he's that focused on his novel, or if he's trying to figure out how to tell me, "Just kidding! Everything I said today was a joke!"

He doesn't stand up and do that, though, so I go to my side of the bed and lay down. He's put the TV on a music station, the volume low, and I wonder if he did that to try to be romantic. Or maybe this is just what he does in the evenings to relax and unwind.

I remind myself that we've been relaxing and unwinding all day long. Food, drinks, snacks, more frozen drinks, the beach, the ocean. It's one long day of relaxation.

Our date didn't happen tonight either, because we couldn't get a reservation at one of the restaurants, and I'm not wearing my heels to a buffet.

After the confession-fest and chips and guac, I found him back on the beach. Different loungers, different mood, different everything.

I hate that everything is different. But I also like it. There's no tension here anymore, and I *need* this to be the relaxing, de-stressing vacation it's always been.

"So jungle hiking and cenote snorkeling tomorrow?" I ask.

The glow moves, and Logan twists his head toward me. "It's not really hiking. It's walking down a gravel road to the cenote."

"We do have to go into the jungle, though."

"Yes, into the jungle."

"Good thing I brought bug spray," I mutter, to which Logan doesn't respond.

"It's half the day, Sloany." The eReader closes, which blots out the light, and he stands with a groan. "We'll be back by one, and we can have lunch and then chill. Shower. Whatever. Dinner is at seven at Café Blanchette."

He takes the step up, an unreadable expression on his face. I've spent all day analyzing every look, every touch, every sound he makes. I'm exhausted, because I'm not a mind-reader, and I can't sit and ask him fifty thousand questions. I'd come off as a psychopath, and I'm trying to avoid that.

I honestly have no idea how to date anymore. It's been so long, and Logan isn't a stranger. I can't ask him the obvious questions, like *do you have any pets,* or *tell me about your family.*

"So we're eating at one and at seven?"

"Sounds like it."

That answer annoys me, but I don't comment on it. My lips purse together as Murph goes into the bathroom and closes the double-doors. I can hear him brushing his teeth, and I'm horrified at what he might've heard me doing in there.

I'd had *quite* the conversation with myself in the shower tonight. His phone rings, and he answers it. His voice is garbled and somewhat quiet, though I can hear it, and I relax. He can't hear me above the shower, even if I talk incessantly.

He laughs, which makes me smile. At the same time, I'm so nervous I can't even move my shoulders. They're pinned up by my ears, and I force myself to take a deep breath, close my eyes, and push the air out of my lungs.

That gets my shoulders down, but the tension now rides in my chest. I have to know what tonight is going to be like. I've been entertaining romantic thoughts about Logan for a couple of days now.

Days.

Not years.

He hasn't kissed me, and I'm not even sure how that's going to go. What if it's like kissing my brother? Not that I have a brother, but if I did. What if there's no spark there at all?

"There is," I assure myself. We'd gone to the buffet tonight, and Murph had helped me out of the golf cart. He put his hand on the small of my back and guided me up the sidewalk, claiming me as his, keeping me close.

I shiver just thinking about it, and I'd definitely felt fireworks when it had happened. "It's going to be fine," I whisper.

I don't want to sleep with him tonight. It's too fast, and I'm still grappling with a lot of things right now. We haven't even been out on our first official date. I shake my head. No. I'm keeping my pajamas on tonight, and so is he.

The doors open, and panic shoots through me. He snaps off the bathroom light and then the main light, which only leaves my lamp burning. He moves with the grace of an athlete as he walks to his side of the bed and pulls his shirt off, dropping it on the nightstand before pulling down the comforter.

"You're staring at me," he says.

"Yeah." I swallow, but the nerves don't go down. "I mean, it's...we're in one bed."

"Yep." He once again sits with his back to me. "We did this last night too."

"So tonight is just going to be like last night?"

"Yep." He lays down and rolls toward me, a smile sliding across his face. "You're on top of the blanket."

I get up and pull down my side of the blanket. Turned away from him, I take a deep breath and switch off the lamp. Darkness plunges into the room, and it's far easier to get into the bed that way.

Logan's hand is warm and soft and insistent as he touches my back. I roll easily toward him, relieved when he tucks me against his chest with a soft sigh. "See?" he whispers. "Just like that."

He moves the comforter around so it's covering both of us, and I dare to slide my hand along his side and up his ribs to his back. He says nothing, and the strong, steady beat of his pulse comforts and lulls me at the same time.

When I wake, Logan isn't in bed. The sun isn't really up either, and I roll toward my side of the bed with a groan just as my alarm goes off. "The whole point of vacation is not to set an alarm," I grumble.

"Snorkeling!" Logan announces as he comes inside from the balcony. "Come on, Sloany. You love snorkeling."

"I hate morning people." I glare at him as I stand and run my hand through my hair. It gets stuck, and I don't even try to get the curls to unsnarl.

He laughs and says, "You're a morning person. I'm

ready, so I'll wait downstairs while you get dressed. We have to be over there in twenty minutes, ready to go."

"I'll be ready to go," I say, mimicking his cheery tone. He grins as he approaches, and he only straightens his lips to press them to my cheek. Then he's gone.

I reach up and touch where he kissed me. It's so unfair that he can render me so shook with something so simple. I can't even imagine what kissing him will be like.

I'm also not sure how much time passes before I lurch into action. I change out of my pajamas quickly and into my swimming suit. For snorkeling, I opt to go with the full body suit, with bright flowers down the side. The rest is black, and I think I look like a million bucks in it.

Feeling like a million bucks takes two minutes of tooth brushing and quickly braiding my hair so it'll stay out of the way no matter what might happen in the cenote. Or on the boat. Or underwater. If I come back from this excursion alive, my hair will still be in that braid.

After that, I quickly pull a cover-up over my head and shimmy it down my body. It barely covers the shorts on the bodysuit, but it'll allow me to enter restaurants and public places without looking like I just washed ashore.

I packed my bag last night, so I grab it and go, don't see Murph loitering in the hall, and head for the elevator. I can hear him laughing downstairs, and sure enough, when I get there, he's entertaining the butlers.

He's got a golf cart waiting too, and he grins at me and takes my hand all in stride. I'm getting quite used to it, actually, and I return his smile without a second thought. Now that I don't have to try to figure out if he feels this bulging, hot thing between us, I don't have to analyze every single smile or look he gives me.

Once I'm seated, Murph takes my pack and goes around to the other side of the golf cart. We jet off toward the main gates of the resort, where we're supposed to meet the van that will take us into the jungles of Belize.

"You look amazing." Murph's breath washes over the side of my neck, sending a chill through my body. His hand slides along my knee and up my leg a little, and I dang near kick out in an involuntary reaction.

I look over to him, and he's got that dangerous look in his eyes. Mine drop to his mouth, and oh my word. I shouldn't have looked there. Now all I can think about is kissing him, and he leans in a little, as if he'll get the job done right now.

He chuckles as he presses his cheek to mine. "You look like I might murder you in the cenote today."

"Do I?" I need to get my game face on, because I don't want this vacation to be lived in fear and panic.

"Yeah," he says. "Like last night when I came over to go to bed." He doesn't miss much, this Logan Murphy. I knew that about him, because out of everyone who'd witnessed me crying and explaining the situation about my loser fiancé who didn't show up for the wedding, *he's* the one who did something.

He's the one who came over. He's the one who acted.

"It's new territory," I say, covering his hand with mine. "Like this. I barely know what to do."

"Mm."

"I hate that humming noise you make."

He bursts out laughing. "Why's that?"

"Because I never know what it means."

"That one meant I was agreeing with you. I barely know what to do either."

"Well, you're—" I clamp my mouth closed, grateful my brain has caught up to the situation.

"I'm what?"

Doing a great job, is what I was going to say.

"You're a natural," I say instead. That's not much better, but at least he won't know how strongly he's affected me.

The golf cart drops us off just outside the gates of the resort, since it doesn't allow cars in. On the street corner, our tour guide is holding a sign, and two other couples hover near him. I shouldn't be surprised, because this is an adults-only resort, and there won't be kids.

I stick to Murph's side, my hand tightly in his, as we approach. He talks to the guide and our names get checked off. A dark gray van rolls to a stop, and he opens the door. "In here," he says. "We're just waiting for one more couple." He scans the area, but it's early, and there isn't anyone around.

We're closest to the van, so Murph steps in first and goes all the way to the back. Fine by me. Then we'll be last out, and if there are any issues at the cenote, maybe we won't die. I nearly hit my head on the ceiling of the van, and by the time I wedge my hips past the seats and collapse onto the back bench seat, I'm sweating.

"I'm so glad we're doing something outdoorsy today," I tell him.

He says nothing but takes my hand again the moment he can. The other two couples sit in the front, and now they're chatting with each other, learning where everyone is from, and all of that. I talk to so many people in my job that I'm completely disinterested in making small talk on a van in the middle of a foreign country. Yeah, we're all in Belize. Big deal.

The last couple never shows, and the tour guide slides the van door closed. There's an empty bench seat between us and the other couples, and I ask, "How long until we get there?"

Murph looks at me like I've lost my mind. "How would I know?"

"I'm going to take a morning nap." I lean my head against his shoulder and close my eyes. Unfortunately, the driver of this party van doesn't seem to realize that it's barely six a.m., and the music blasts through the speakers.

I jerk my head up, blinking. I'm going to have a raging headache by the time we get to the end of the block. I think for sure someone will say something about the pounding beat, but no one does. Not even Murph.

He keeps me close to his side, and I can admit it's

where I want to be anyway. He bends his head toward me, and I tilt my ear up to be able to hear him. "When did you decide you might want to go out with me?"

My lungs freeze mid-breath. I can't tell him the moment I saw him standing at the baggage claim in Atlanta, can I?

Why not?

I duck my head, seeing him in my mind's eye.

"In Atlanta," I say. "I saw you at the baggage claim before you turned around, and I don't know. I've been thinking about getting back into the boxing ring, and I thought—maybe with Murph."

"The boxing ring?"

"Dating again."

"You've been thinking about dating again? Before I mentioned it?"

I nod. "Yeah. I mean, a little. I wasn't actually going to do it."

"No?"

"Who am I going to go out with in Pittsburgh?" I turn and look at him. "For real?"

"I don't know. I'm sure the city is full of single men."

"Single for a reason." I face the front again, glad now that the music is so loud. It's insulating this conversation from the other couples.

"I'm single."

"For a reason."

"What would that reason be?"

I meet Murph's eyes again, and his sparkle like stars. He's teasing me, but I think he has a valid question. "Why *are* you single?" I ask. "You could've gone out with anyone in Superior."

"I didn't want to go out with anyone in Superior," he says. He finally looks away. "I guess that's my reason for being single."

"Me?" I ask. "*I'm* the reason you're still single?"

"For the past couple of years, yeah," he says. "Let's talk about something else, please."

"Oh, now you want to talk about something else?"

Blue fire burns in his eyes as he trains them on me again. "Yes." His shutters are back in place, and that irritates me. I don't know what he's thinking, but it's probably something about how slow I am to come to the conclusion that it's time to move on.

I look away from him too, my thoughts growing teeth and then more. There's little I hate more than wasting my time. I wish Murph would've said something a couple of trips ago, because then maybe we'd be getting close to getting engaged instead of just starting out.

The sky begins to lighten, and I take in the wonder around me. The city is gone, and the trees of the jungle press close to the edge of the road. They blur by so fast that I close my eyes and turn away.

I squeeze Murph's hand, and he turns toward me. "I'm excited about this."

"Are you?"

"Yeah." I snuggle into his side. "Thanks for booking this for us." On all of our trips, he's always handled the details. The day trips. The meals. All of it. Probably because on that first non-honeymoon we took, I was a blubbering mess who barely left the room except when he told me I had to.

I barely remember that trip. The only thing that lingers in my memory is how much I appreciated Logan Murphy for not letting me go alone.

The driver turns the van down a dirt road, and a parking lot holds back the trees. To my surprise, a couple of other vans are already there, and it feels like we're arriving a little bit late.

Our guide opens the door and says, "Come with me, please."

I wait for the other couples to get out and follow him, and then I do the same. We get fins and snorkeling gear, all the while the guide telling us about cenotes and the waterways in Belize, Mexico, and other Central American countries.

"So it's a sinkhole," I whisper to Murph. "We're literally going to be diving into an unstable land formation."

"They're stable now," he says.

"Mm." I really enunciate it, but there's no way I can make my timbre match his. He still gets the message and rolls his eyes, though a smile plays with the corners of his mouth.

"Come, please," our guide calls.

"Stop making us late," Murph teases.

"Are you kidding me right now?" I glare at him, but it's all in jest. I'm super glad I wore the shorts, so my thighs aren't rubbing together on this walk down the dirt path. It's wide enough for two or three people, so Murph walks at my side. He barely seems to be moving, but I'm pushing myself to a near speed-walk.

We catch up to our group, and the guide gives us directions for the cenote. "Explore the edges," he says. "The fish like to hide in the rocks. We'll be here about twenty minutes, and then we'll go do the underground cave."

I say nothing, though I'm screaming *underground cave?* in my head. I've been snorkeling before, as this isn't my first time to a tropical location. With my snorkel attached to the band on my goggles, I slip them over my head, beyond glad I braided my hair. Otherwise, this strap would pull out so much hair, and I'd be cursing Logan's name so loud.

"You need a haircut," I say when I look at him. He's already put his mask over his nose and mouth, but mine is perched on my forehead.

"Do I?"

"It's curling." I reach up and touch it. "There's a barber at the resort."

His hand lands on my hip, and every other nerve cell in my body dies. Only the ones where he touches fire, and they're going off like cannons. "I thought you liked my hair longer."

"I—" I told him that the last time he sent me a picture. He said he had to send something to his sister, and he'd wanted to know which one. I'd gotten three options in my text messages, and I'd chosen the one where he'd looked the happiest.

When he'd asked me why I'd picked that one, I said I'd liked it the best because his hair was a little longer.

I clear my throat. "I do like your hair a little longer."

"Mm."

I nudge his ribs with my elbow, and he laughs as he dances away. "You're so funny," I say, bringing my goggles down and into position. "Come on. Everyone else has gotten in already, and the clock is ticking."

I sit down on the bridge, my feet going into the water. Though it's still pretty early in the morning, the water is warm, and I pull my fins on. Once Murph is ready to go, we look at each other, stick our snorkels in our mouths, and jump in together.

Every time I snorkel, I have a panic attack in the first few seconds. My brain yells at me that we're a human being, not a fish, and we can't breathe underwater.

I pop right back up, gasping. I pull the mouthpiece out and take a deep breath as I calm my fight or flight response. I sputter and shake the water from the snorkel. Then I bite on the mouthpiece, take a deep breath, and face-in I go.

Calmly, I breathe out, then back in, and the only sound in the world is the steady, Darth-Vader-like in and out of my own breath. I love it. I love being able to see what's beneath the surface of the water. I love snorkeling with my whole soul.

I kick with the fins, and swimming is suddenly easy for someone who's a non-swimmer. I stick to the edge the way the guide said to, and I see a handful of silver-gray fish with black stripes. Joy fills me, and I look around for someone to share it with.

Logan is right there, and I point. He gives me a thumbs up, because there's no talking underwater. I stay near him, and we make our way around the cenote, taking in the vibrant life in the part-salt water and part-fresh water environment.

There isn't anything super bright or tropical, because we're not in the ocean. It doesn't matter. Seeing an environment I haven't before makes me see with new eyes, and I come up back at the bridge with the biggest smile on my face.

I've never been great at boosting myself out of a swimming pool, but thankfully, there's a ladder. I doggy paddle over to it as Murph surfaces.

"Are we getting out?"

"They're all out," I say, nodding to the bridge. The other couples in our group are just hanging out, their legs dangling into the water, but I still feel like Murph and I are the problem children of the group.

He follows me over to the ladder, and I miss finding the bottom step a couple of times before my foot lands on it. I start to pull myself up, but apparently, I've forgotten how to climb a ladder, and I lose my balance.

"Whoa." I start to fall backward, and then two palms push right against my backside. Murph's palms.

Embarrassment floods me from head to toe, but he manages to get me back on track. I grunt as I scramble up the few steps to the wood.

Murph, of course, swam in high school and college and emerges from the cenote like an Olympian. He shakes that long hair as if he's in a cologne commercial and grins at me.

"You're really annoying," I say.

His smile fades. "Why?"

"You literally smashed my butt with your hands."

"I didn't want you to fall on me."

"And then you climb out of the cenote and shake your fabulous hair like you just won Gold."

He blinks, and I swat at his chest. He pulls back, but I still make contact with his skin. "I didn't want you to fall on me." I shake my head and walk away. "Nothing any woman wants to hear, ever."

I grab my towel from where I draped it over a tree, and I look around for the guide. He's coming toward us, thankfully, and he calls everyone together. Murph comes to my side, his eyes like a puppy dog seeking forgiveness.

I give him a cold shoulder and follow the guide further

into the forest. The path only accommodates one person at a time, and I'm near the front of our group now. We reach the underground cenote, though some of the black water can be seen lapping against the gray rocks.

"We're going in there?" I ask.

"It'll be dark," the guide says. "There are a few guides wearing headlamps, and we have some spotlights anchored in the ground too. You won't see any life in this underground cenote, because there's no saltwater in them. It's a dead system, but you'll be able to see the rock formations from long ago."

A woman screams behind him, and we all look that direction. She comes up sputtering, her voice loud as she says, "It's freezing."

The guide faces us and smiles. "It is a little cold getting in. Then it's not too bad. Be sure to get your picture taken against the back wall."

The couple in front of me goes first, and then Murph and I crowd onto the small platform where people are getting in and out of the cenote. "Let's be sure to get a picture, okay?" he asks. "Or are you too annoyed with me?"

"Oh, you're fine," I say. "I'm sure you could tow me over there if I drown." I give him a withering look, then step into the water. I gasp at the temperature, but people are waiting to get in and out, so I don't have a choice.

In I go.

I feel the same way about starting a romantic relationship with Logan—like I'm stepping into cold, dark water, with only a wing and a prayer that I'll survive.

There might be some spotlights at various places, but it'll be mostly dark. Dark and cold, with only a guide at the end of it, after the outcome is already known. The unknown already explored.

The stakes are so much higher than just me, though. It's *us*. It's trips like this. It's a friendship I value above anything else.

I come up from the water in the cenote sputtering, a chill moving through me.

Chapter Eleven
Sloane

I step into my heels just as the doorbell on the room rings. A smile touches my heart and soul and seeps onto my face. Logan had gotten ready a half hour ago and left to give me space to prepare for our date tonight—and to be able to come "pick me up properly."

I pause in the double doors of the bathroom and check myself one final time. Makeup: flawless. My form-fitting dark blue dress: perfect. Jewelry: complementary. The bright red heels: sexy—and patriotic when paired with the blue dress, if I do say so myself.

I'm not good at everything, but I know how to put myself together so that I'm absolutely flawless. I do it five days a week for my job, and hopefully, this will be the only time I do the same thing here on our vacation.

We always pack one fancier outfit and go somewhere really high-end. The resorts we've stayed at have five-star restaurants where beachwear isn't even allowed, so this is a tradition.

At the same time, it's also a first. Because it hasn't been a date-date before. It's just us playing dress-up and going out like we're fancy when we're not.

I take a deep breath, sucking in my stomach. My chest sticks out further, and I glance down to check the coverage of my dress. I'm only showing the slightest amount of cleavage, which is how I like to be. Subtle sexy. Tease with a taste, and let him imagine the rest.

Satisfied that I've accomplished what I intend to, I step over to the door and open it. My breath catches in my throat at the sight of Logan standing in the hallway.

He's holding a dozen deep, dark red roses, and I suddenly feel like light is beaming from my face the way the spotlights did from deep inside the dark cenote.

He's wearing his slacks, paired with a light blue dress shirt and a pair of loafers. He doesn't normally wear a tie, and he didn't have one around his neck when he left.

Now he does. It's black and white and gold, and it somehow feels exactly like something he would've brought with him from Superior.

His eyes dance with happiness and light, and they drip down my body. He doesn't whistle. He doesn't pay any compliments verbally. The hunger in his expression says it all.

"Where did you get these?" I take the roses from him and lean down to inhale their heady, velvety scent.

"A man has to have some secrets," he says.

I turn to put the flowers in the room, and I quickly return to the door. Murph takes me into his arms, his voice husky and nearly hoarse as he says, "I'm the luckiest man in the country."

"Just the country?"

"The whole continent." His lips nip along my earlobe, and my eyes fall closed in anticipation of more. But he pulls back and whispers, "We can't be late for our reservation, sweetheart."

"No, sir," I manage to push out my narrow throat.

"Our golf cart awaits." He steps away and offers me his arm.

I slip my elbow through his. "Where'd you get that tie?"

"Gift shop," he says. "I spied it yesterday, and I went back just now. I barely made it, because they close at six-thirty."

"It's nice."

"Thanks, I thought so too."

It's dusky outside already, and it'll be full dark in a matter of minutes. Tea lights hang in the railings and banisters of the first floor, making everything feel magical and tropical at the same time.

Murph waits for me to sit in the golf cart before rounding it to join me, where he takes my hand in his. "Spa day tomorrow," he says.

"You sure you want to come do the massage?"

"Of course," he says. "You'll get your nails done in the morning, and I'll join you just before lunch. The beach after that."

"Your whole day is planned," I tease. "How will you survive?"

He doesn't answer as he shakes his head, and I wonder what he's thinking. Hopefully how cute and playful I am. How easy I am to talk to would also be acceptable.

We get to the restaurant, which has more lights and the light, twinkling sounds of classical music playing in the speakers outside where the line is for golf carts. Inside, it's busy, but they move people through the line and to their tables for the seven o'clock reservation really quickly.

I lay my napkin over my lap while a waitress dressed in black from head to toe pours wine into my glass. Murph says he'd like a Tom Collins, and I raise my eyebrows at him. He simply lifts both hands as if to say, *What can I say?*

Once we're alone, I lean forward and put my arms on the table. "Tom Collins?"

"I'm allowed to drink on vacation."

"I didn't say you weren't." I lift my wine glass and give it a swirl. "You usually don't, though."

"It's a special night." He picks up the slip of paper that's the menu. At fancy resorts like this, there's usually one or two choices per course, and we can order all of it if we want to. "Carrot ginger soup," he reads. "French onion soup. Gotta have that."

"We should get one of each," I say.

"One of everything." This isn't a new game for us, as we've eaten together at restaurants like this several times in the past. Murph is right, though. Tonight is a special night.

That decided, I set down my wine and focus on him. "Tell me what you remember about our first trip together."

Alarm pulls across his face. He shifts in his seat as he abandons the menu. "Our first trip? Why do you want to talk about that?"

"I don't remember a lot of it," I say honestly. "I can't have been much fun."

"You were just fine."

"What do you remember?" I ask again.

Murph looks like he wants to disappear from the table, and I regret bringing up this topic. I sure do know how to kill the mood. I look down as the waitress appears with his drink. "Are you ready to order?" she asks.

"Yes," Murph says smoothly. "We want one of everything." He hands her his slip of paper, and I do the same. She nods, takes them, and leaves.

"Never mind," I say, knowing he'll be able to keep up with the non-conversation we've been having. "I don't want to know."

"I remember you being brave," he says in that quiet, authoritative way he has. I would never contradict him that I'm not brave. "And so put together. You'd literally just been stood up at the altar and made the trip to the airport yourself, and you hadn't forgotten to pack anything."

"That's because I packed before the wedding," I say.

"You had a first aid kit."

I smile and duck my head. "Yes, but I forgot I had it, remember? You cut your foot on those rocks, and I freaked out."

"You didn't freak out." He picks up my hand and plays with my fingers. "You just don't like the sight of blood. I learned that about you too."

"I had the first aid kit yesterday too," I say. "It's stupid I never remember I have it, because I go into blood-shock."

"Yeah, you had to wear that Hello Kitty Band-aid for like, five minutes."

"You're irritating me."

"No, I'm not."

No, he's not. My default is to keep asking him questions. Keep him talking. I remind myself that it's okay to allow for some silence too, because Murph and I aren't near-strangers. I tell myself to stay silent and let him come up with something he wants to know about me that he doesn't already.

"How's your mom?" he asks, and I shouldn't be surprised at the question. I've told him all the drama between my parents.

But I don't want to talk about them on this trip. "We're on vacation," I say. "Real life doesn't exist."

Something shutters over his eyes, but he says, "Fair

enough," and then we're both distracted by the soup course.

"Wow," he says, gazing down at the creamy, browned cheese melted over the rim of the dark black bowl in front of him.

"I didn't even know they made pottery that color," I marvel. This is the ritziest resort we've ever stayed at, and I have to admit I'm not upset about it.

"Yours is so pretty too," he says, peering over to my bowl. My soup—the carrot ginger—is the brightest orange I've ever seen. The bowl is easily as big as a dinner plate and maybe an inch or two deep. Candied ginger swims in the middle of it, and something white and something bright green has been swirled on top of the soup.

I look up, wonder streaming through me. "This is the first course," I say.

"I'll save you a crouton." He takes the first bite of soup, and he's got miles and miles of Swiss cheese stringing down, and only a few croutons pop up from under the cheesy top. He moans, and it's a completely different type of sound than that hum he makes.

We share the soup back and forth, and when we've scooped up every last drop of both bowls, I lean back, already satisfied. "Okay, what was the winner?"

"Yours," he says.

"Really? We're at the French restaurant, and the French onion soup didn't win?"

He lifts one sexy, confident shoulder and says, "I've had better."

I laugh, because such a statement is so Murph. Logan. Logan Murphy. My chest expands in such a comfortable, amazing way, and I reach over and twine my fingers with his.

"Thank you for this," I say. "It's lovely. This place—the resort. This dinner. Us."

He lifts my hand to his lips and touches them there. "Us." His eyes sparkle like fireworks in the deepest, darkest sky, a blanket that holds everything where it needs to be.

The main course arrives, and I pull my hand back as two women slide two plates onto our table. "Steak au Poivre," one of them says. That plate goes in front of Logan, and it contains some medium-rare steak with a gorgeous, glossy red wine sauce spooned over the top.

Four potatoes decorate the plate, and they have sprinkles of greenery on them. Dollops of condiments line the top rim of the plate, and Logan gazes at it like he's seen the most wonderful thing in the world.

"Stuffed pork tenderloin," the other woman says, and I get meat candy placed in front of me. It's been rolled with a filling of cheese, apples, and greens inside, and an icing of glazed bacon rings the whole thing.

I pull my plate a little closer to me, because I've got a fluffy pile of mashed potatoes with my pork, my mouth watering though I'd thought the soup was the best thing I'd eaten, ever.

The waitresses leave, and Logan and I look at each other. "We should go somewhere nice like this every year," I say.

He chuckles and says, "Okay," without a single question.

"I'll start saving right now for next year," I say as I lift my knife from the plate. I slice off a triangle of the pork, bringing the filling out from the middle, and put the whole thing in my mouth.

My reaction to the moist meat, the tart cheese and apples, the savory greens, and that sweet and salty bacon... My eyes roll back in my head, and I'm so glad my mouth and teeth know how to chew and swallow.

"My tongue is so happy," I say.

Logan grins as he puts a bite of steak in his mouth. "Mm, yes." He likes red meat more than I do, but we share the main courses, him eating more of the steak and me eating more of the pork.

"Winner?" he asks.

"Pork," I say. "Obviously."

"Steak," he says. "Obviously."

We grin at each other, and I don't think I've ever been on a better date. The waitresses give us time to chat and watch the tea lights floating along the river that lines the path that leads down to the pool and then the beach.

Finally, coffee is brought with our desserts, and I've

never seen the most perfect crunchy caramel topping on the crème brûlée. I can't wait to crack that with my spoon; I can hear the sound of it in my ears already.

Logan has a chocolate soufflé that lifts a good three inches above the top of his ramekin, and he looks at it like a starving man looking at Thanksgiving dinner.

"Wow," he says again, and I agree.

"One," I say, lifting my spoon. "Two. Three." I crack my spoon against the hard caramel, and it splinters in the most satisfying way.

Logan dives into his soufflé and says, "This is the lightest thing I've ever seen." He puts the light brown bite in his mouth, and I scoop up some creamy crème with a shard of caramel and taste it against my tongue.

It's smooth. It's delicate. It's perfectly room temperature, with that tang of the eggs with the sweetness of the vanilla. "This is so good."

The desserts disappear quickly, and I lean back to rest my hands on my stomach. "I'm so full. I think this is the best meal I've ever eaten."

Logan only smiles at me, because he's a cook. He actually likes it, something I don't fathom. "Could you make me something like this?" I ask.

"I could, sure," he says. "Maybe not that soufflé. That was incredible."

"It was." We linger over coffee, my mind moving through all kinds of different scenarios for what might happen when we get back to the room.

We opt to walk back to our building to get our food to settle a little bit, and I saunter along at his side, my arm laced lazily through his. We don't talk, and the peacefulness of the resort here coats me in such a layer of comfort.

He unlocks the door and lets me enter first, and I glance at him as I do. I pause and put my hand against his chest. "Thank you, Logan. This was the most perfect date ever."

I tip up and sweep my lips along his cheek and then enter the room. I kick off my heels with a sigh, and when I don't hear the door close, I turn back to him.

He's standing there watching me, pure fondness on his face. He catches me staring, and he quickly enters the honeymoon suite and lets the door close.

"It was a great first date," he agrees as he starts to remove his tie. Standing in this room with him while we start to undo all the parts we've put together for each other is incredibly intimate, and I quickly gather my shower things and duck into the bathroom.

I didn't kiss him, and I ask the rainfall water why as I stand under it. But the shower water doesn't know. Maybe I'm just not ready. Maybe because I never kiss on the first date.

"Maybe tomorrow," I whisper to myself.

"Look." I show Murph my beautiful ruby-red fingernails as we're walking down the hall.

"Nice." He gives me a smile and focuses in front of him again.

We're following a man and a woman, but neither of them are wearing white, fluffy robes with nothing underneath the way we are. We'd only waited together for about five minutes, wherein Murph told me he did, in fact, enjoy running on the beach while I got my nails done.

His hair is damp, as he showered here before our massage, and I want to run my hands through it just to see how silky it is while wet.

My heart pounds as the attendants turn a corner. "You know we'll be on the table at the same time, right?"

"You told me this morning," he says.

"You're going to get on first," I say, because I can't stop myself. "I'll face the corner and close my eyes."

"Mm."

"Do not hum at me, Logan."

"Yes," he says. "I'm going to get on the table first, with you facing the corner and your eyes closed." He catches my hand on the next swing. "I was agreeing with you."

"I can't distinguish your hums yet."

"Why are you nervous about this?"

"Because I'm not wearing any clothes under my robe?" I look at him, dumbfounded. "Why are you *not* nervous about this?"

"Maybe because I've been holding you in my arms for the past three nights, and I'm half-naked already?"

"Yeah, but *I'm* not."

His eyebrows go up.

"What?" I ask. His face pinks up, and it's absolutely delicious. I nudge him with my hip. "What?"

"You're not wearing a bra at night," he says, that dark grin appearing.

"You dirty man," I say, tugging my hand away.

He chuckles. "Come on. I'm not dirty. I'm just a man."

"Sure."

"Do you not want me to find you desirable physically?"

"I mean—no."

"No, you don't? Or no, you don't not want me to?"

"You're confusing me."

"Sure, I am." He squeezes my hand. "Besides, I've seen you in a bikini, and that's almost like what you *don't* have on under your robe."

"It is not." I roll my eyes. "It's not the same at all."

"What are you wearing to the beach this afternoon?" he challenges.

"The red bra," I tell him, just now deciding.

"See? Almost nothing."

I choose not to respond, because our attendants are waiting in a doorway, smiling like we're about to have the time of our lives. Murph makes me go first, and I choose the table away from the door. It looks like a regular massage table, and while I don't have regular massages, I have had them before. Nothing special about this one, other than the fact that there's another one only five feet from it.

I swallow and focus on the man as he closes the door. "Welcome," he says in the semi-darkness. "Any issues we need to know about?"

Murph launches into this hotspot in his right calf and how, when he runs, something in his back has been pulling lately. I wave off my therapist, because I don't have any issues. Not any I'm going to confess to in front of Murph, anyway.

"We'll let you get settled in," the man says. "Face-down to start, please." They both leave, and I can't look at Murph. I spin and face the wall, my eyes pressed closed.

"No peeking," he teases.

"I hate you," I say.

"No, you don't." The sound of rustling sheets fills the room, and then the movement of the table. More rustling, and I swear it takes him a decade to say, "Okay, Sloany. Your turn."

I turn slowly just to make sure he's down and covered. He is, so I shed my robe and hang it on the nearby hook. Standing naked in the room, I feel the chill of the air and glance at Murph.

He's face-down, and he doesn't so much as have a muscle spasm. I quickly peel back the thin blanket and climb on the table. Mine makes so much more noise than

Murph's, and I grit my teeth as I lower myself and then fit my face into the headpiece.

It takes me a minute to get the blanket up over my shoulders, and I swear I grunt and almost throw my shoulder out of its socket in the process. Murph mercifully says nothing. I've barely stopped moving, and I'm sweating and breathing hard when someone knocks on the door.

"Ready?" he asks, his voice tickling my eardrums.

"Yes."

"Okay," he calls, and the two attendants enter the room. I try to relax, but I'm seriously regretting having a couples massage. I don't want to talk to anyone during my spa services, and surely Murph and I won't carry on a conversation in front of strangers. So why are we here together? He could be enjoying his massage and me mine in two separate rooms.

My therapist pulls the blanket back, letting the cooler air kiss my back. I pull in a breath, hold it, and then release it slowly. By controlling my breathing, I can control my thoughts, and I finally get them all corralled as a pair of strong, capable hands moves down the length of my spine.

Ohhh, yeahhh. This is what I want. The table beneath me is heated, and I just start to notice it on the second stroke of her hands. Time holds no meaning during a massage. I let go of all of my worries too, and when she says, "Roll over and move down, please," I do it without thinking too hard.

One, Murph has already done it, and two, I'm not sure

I care at this juncture. She's relaxed me to that point, and that is a true miracle.

We finish within seconds of each other, and my therapist drapes my robe over my shins. "I'll have some water outside," she says.

"Mm." I don't even care that I've just turned into Murph. I keep my eyes closed, because I don't want to acknowledge that this massage is over. The door clicks closed, though, and I can't lay here forever.

"Do you want to get up first?" he asks.

"No," I moan.

He chuckles as he gets up, the sounds of his table telling me to stay right where I am. "I'm good," he says. "I'll see you in the hall."

The door opens and closes again, and I finally allow myself to open my eyes. The room is as dim as ever, and I feel like I can barely move. I really need to find a masseuse in Pittsburgh and achieve this level of relaxation monthly.

I get up and cover up in the robe, knotting the ties extra-tight. When I emerge from the room, it seems wrong that there's so much bright light in the hall. The world has gone on while I got rubbed down.

"Good?" my attendant asks, handing me a bottle of water.

"So good." I twist the cap and take a drink. Murph grins at me from down the hall, and I head his way. "How was your massage?"

"Magical," he says.

I peer at him. "Are you making fun of me?"

"You moan a lot during a massage," he says. "Did you know?"

"Shut up," I say. "I do not." I glance over to my therapist, and she gives me a small smile that says I absolutely moaned a lot.

Great. Just great. "Well, it was a really good massage." I hold my head high all the way back to the waiting room, where Murph and I will separate to go get dressed. My therapist leaves, and I'm about to as well when Murph grabs my hand. I face him again. "What?"

"At least now I know what sound I hope to hear when I finally kiss you." With that, he releases my hand, salutes me—the nerve!—and pushes into the men's dressing room.

Chapter Twelve
Logan

I put the phone on speaker and run the towel through my hair. Sloane's gone down to the beach already to secure us a place for Tiki Night, leaving me to get a few things done for work and talk to my mom.

I wait for her to finish the tale about the water heater. "So you got it fixed?" I finally ask, because she never did say.

"Yes," she says with a sigh. "Lenny came last night, and the water's piping hot this morning."

"That's great, Mom." A tiny twinge of guilt that I wasn't there to help rings through me. "You got into my place okay?"

"Yes," she says. "You had a ton of mail. A great big box I had your father haul in for you."

I frown as I reach for my third of three pairs of swim trunks I brought. I comment every day on Sloane's swimwear, and the pink bra top was...spectacular. My mouth turns dry at the thought of it.

She'll probably wear it again, because she said she ended up only bringing six suits, and we're here for ten nights and nine days. She barely wears real clothes, even if we're not on the beach. She's got a few outfits for our evening meals, but even then, she's worn a coverup dress over her suit in the past.

"A great big box?" I ask. "What was it?"

"I don't know, dear. Dad brought it in and left it by the front door. We're supposed to get eight inches this week."

I shudder just thinking about the snow. Why I live so far north is a mystery to me. I'm self-employed and work from home. I don't have to be anywhere near Wisconsin.

"Mom," I start as I pull on my trunks. But I suddenly remember what's in the box. "Oh, those are my author copies from Destiny."

"Author copies?"

"I have to go, Mom." I lunge toward the phone and tap the red icon. I hear her start to say something, and I press my eyes closed. Yep, definitely a bad son.

Keeping secrets from my mother. She doesn't know I'm a romance novelist, nor that I'm planning on leaving Superior. I'd been about to tell her one of those, then blurted out the other.

"Stupid." I shake my head, because I have to handle this delicately, especially the leaving Superior bit. I can't just blurt it out in paragraphs of text the way I did with my suppressed feelings for Sloane.

"Sloane."

I don't know what to do about her either. We spent a great day at the spa, then she had the butler fill the balcony jacuzzi with rose petals and hot water. She kept asking me to join her, but I didn't.

I don't trust myself around her. And put her in that bra top and rose-scented water, on a private balcony? She'd cuddle into me, nearly naked, and I'd want to get her all the way there.

I haven't kissed her on the mouth yet, and I don't know how to do that either. I feel like I need a plan, and for someone who literally writes entire novels without an outline and who'd rather go out spur of the moment than make plans, that's a big deal.

"Plan," I mutter to myself. "Plan, plan, plan." I slide my feet into my flip flops and pick up my keycard. I don't need a wallet or cash, so my phone goes in my pocket, and I'm ready to leave.

Sloane will have sunscreen, but the sun's almost down. She left her bag here, her parting words, "I've got a key and my party panties on."

Her eyes had danced with mischief, and that means she's going to drink a lot of margaritas tonight. I'll be her designated roomie, and that's fine with me. I lose my head with more than one drink in me, and I'm determined not to do that with Sloane.

"Come down ready to keep me company," she'd told me. I'm not entirely sure what she means by that, because I feel like I'm always ready to party.

She and I, we complement each other. Sometimes I'm the quiet one in a crowd, and sometimes she is. It's always worked out that one of us can carry the conversation while the other doesn't feel like it, or we simply don't go out.

I can't imagine this will be a raver or anything. It's an adults-only resort, and I'm pretty sure Sloane and I are two of the youngest people here.

I leave the room and head downstairs, my thoughts on yesterday's guacamole demonstration and tasting. Both Sloane and I had agreed that it wasn't anything special, but there's nothing like fresh guacamole and chips —poolside.

I'd booked us a wine tasting aboard a sailboat for last night's sunset, and that had elicited some excitement from Sloane. But with about a dozen people on-board, and then the chatter back to the room, no opportunity to kiss her had presented itself.

I've never been all that great at seizing opportunities when they come, despite my sister's insistence that I'm one of the luckiest people she knows.

I step onto the sand to a dance party where no one is dancing. Men and women hover around the perimeter of the tiki-marked dance floor, everyone with a glass of something in their hand.

"Murph!" Sloane waves her hand from across the way,

and I lift mine to indicate that I see her. Her cover-up tonight is white, and it makes her look like an angel. She's be-bopping to the music, one of the only people adding some sway to their hips.

Torches burn every few feet, making the area well-lit. There's more people here than I thought there would be, most of them clustered around the chest-high tables closest to the open bar. The mood is ripe for a party, but I'm not sure one will get too far off the ground.

I step off the sidewalk and out onto the dance floor. It feels like every eye within fifty miles zeroes in on me—*he dared to step onto the dance floor! What's going to happen next?*—but I keep my gaze on my destination.

Sloane.

She turns her back on me for a few moments, and when she faces me, she's got a plastic cup of cola in her hand. I step out of the spotlight and back onto safer ground. "That better have a lemon in it."

"It does."

I spy the wedge when I relieve her of the cup, and if it's Diet Coke and not Diet Pepsi I'll be stunned. I had to drive off the property on our non-honeymoon in Mexico to get the right cola, and Sloane's teased me about it ever since.

After taking a sip of the drink, a burn slides down my throat. "This has rum in it."

Sloane gives me a wicked look. "It's tiki night."

I smile, the fire in my throat receding already. So she

didn't have them put much alcohol in it. Fair enough. I'll be fine with this one drink.

"No one's dancing," I say.

"Do you want to lead us out?" Sloane can't stop smiling, and I wonder how many drinks she's had. She currently holds a margarita, the liquid sloshing from side to side as she continues to jive. It's very full, which means she hasn't had much of this one.

I shake my head and say, "No," with a laugh as she pushes against my chest a little. I stumble back a step or two, nowhere near getting back on the dance floor. A new song starts, this one upbeat and sure to make the party take off. Still no one makes a move to be the first one to get wild out in the cleared area.

Waiters and waitresses move through the area, and I take an empanada from a tray. "That's fish," Sloane says like a warning.

"I like fish."

"Your funeral."

The empanada is bite-sized, and I pop the whole thing into my mouth. It probably should've been eaten in two bites, but I don't care. The dough is tender and sweet, and there's some sort of flaked fish in the cream cheese mixture inside. It's not terrible, but it's not great either.

"I won't die," I tell Sloane, who's watching me for my reaction. "But I'm not eating another one."

"There it is." She grins and wraps her arms around my neck. "I want to dance with you."

I steady her with my hands on her hips and say, "Don't dump that drink down my back."

She reaches out and sets it on the table. When she looks at me again, she's wearing eyes that say, *Dance with me, Murph. Kiss me, Murph.*

I want to do both, but only one of them will happen with all these people watching. All this light. My pulse hammers against my Adam's apple, because while I'd like to believe I'm a good kisser, what if Sloane doesn't think I am?

What if, when I finally touch my lips to hers, it's... weird? Or worse, gross?

I'll have to find another place to stay, that's for sure. That means repacking and moving. It means a horribly awkward conversation with Sloane, and then five more days of awfulness. It might be better if I just wait until we're back in Atlanta, ready to separate to our respective cities, to kiss her.

Then, if it's terrible, I can stare longingly out the window as I return to Wisconsin, and she can text her sisters from her gate about what a terrible mistake she made in Belize.

I sway with her, leaning down to touch my forehead to hers. We're not moving fast enough for the music, but then, it hardly matters. There are no rules for this dance party. I also don't move too far from the tables, and Sloane doesn't try to take us out into the public eye either. She knows I won't like that, and then I'll stop dancing with her.

Bringing her closer, I slide my face alongside hers and whisper, "Your cover-up is transparent. Did you know?"

She giggles and doesn't answer. The song ends, and I naturally step back. I have half a mind to clear my throat, but I force myself to refrain. If I make the humming noise, Sloane might find someone else to dance with.

I never realized how often I did that until this trip. Sometimes I do it just to annoy Hattie—and now Sloane— but I don't want to be irritating right now. I glance around, and I see burning lights leading away from the party.

Picking up her drink, I turn. "Come on."

"Come on where?" Sloane comes with me, even if she doesn't want to. "Murph, the party is here."

"No, it isn't."

"Murph."

I break free from the crowd and see the torches lead down to the water. Loungers have been placed there, and both Sloane and I are still wearing our swimming suits. "Look. We can have a more...private party down here."

Sloane doesn't respond to that, and there's decidedly less people here. In fact, we're the only ones. There're only six seats, and I take the one on the end and wait for Sloane to sit next to me before I hand her the margarita.

She smiles and takes a sip before setting it in the sand. "Scootch over."

Before I know it, she's standing and coming over to my lounge chair. I nearly drop my drink in the sand in my haste to make room for her, and instead of sitting next to me, Sloane settles between my legs, her back against my chest.

I easily wrap my arms around her, our fingers lacing together over her stomach. "How many margaritas have you had?"

"Just one," she says. "That's my second one."

"You don't want to dance."

"Mm, no." She snuggles back further. "I want to sit right here and listen to the ocean."

"What's she telling you?"

Sloane sighs, her fingers tightening around mine. "I don't know. I just like listening to her."

I consider the waves lapping at the legs of the chair. The tiki torches flicker against the tips of the water, but the light only casts itself a few feet before it peters out. Further out, pure blackness stares back at us, and lines from a possible book enter my head.

"I think she might tell someone to be brave," I say quietly. "That she moves forward and back, pushes and pulls, never stops. Over rocks and cliffs. It allows boats and ships to part it, but when she gets angry, she lashes back at anything and everything."

"What makes her angry?" Sloane asks.

"Imbalances in the atmosphere, mostly," I say with a smile. "Other than that, she keeps her secrets buried deep. She hides huge mammals, and one-sided fish can blend into the bottom, never to be seen again."

"She does hide a lot of things."

"Like shipwrecks filled with treasure from hundreds of years ago."

"Those squid-octopi that spit ink. The giant ones no one ever sees."

"Animals that look like rocks," I say.

"Some of them look like brains."

I chuckle. "That they do."

She turns slightly in my arms. "You're a good story-teller. You have a nice voice for it."

"Thanks." I smile down at her, and this feels like the moment. The moment I can kiss her, and our fate will be known. A round of giggling interrupts us, and we both glance over to another couple. They're probably a decade older than us, and they've both clearly had too much to drink.

The man stumbles and kicks a lounger a couple away from us, saying, "Whoopsie," like that's a normal thing for a forty-year-old male to utter, and looks over to us. "Sorry," he slurs out next.

They settle on a lounger on the other end, but the moment between Sloane and I is broken. She sighs and settles back against my chest again, and helplessness fills me.

Stupid, I say to myself. I shouldn't have hesitated. I should be making out with Sloane right now, and every muscle in my body is tight with want. With *need*.

"Do you like audiobooks?" I ask, my voice hardly my own.

"What?"

"You like to read," I say. "You said I have a nice voice for narrating stories." I'm on thin ice now, and I tell myself I want to tell Sloane about my job. What I really do with my time. I just don't have the words quite yet—I can't even tell my mom.

"I've never tried audiobooks," she says. "I suppose I should, what with how much I drive around for showings."

"It'd be a lot of starting and stopping," I say. "You wouldn't even come in from the hot tub last night until you finished your book." I'd been both pleased and irritated. I'd gone to bed alone, but of course I was awake when she finally came in, toweled off, showered, and sank into my arms.

She'd fallen asleep in two breaths, though she's often accused me of doing that. I, of course, had lain there for a while. Long enough to get my pulse to calm the heck down and my mind to soften. I'd finally fallen asleep, the petally scent of Sloane's shampoo luring me into slumber.

"It was a good book," she says.

"Why did you like it?"

She tilts her head like she didn't hear me and doesn't answer. She doesn't know that only makes me like her more. In the dark, with the symphony of the ocean so close, maybe I can ask her about this.

I've teased her about her love of romance novels, but

now, I really want to know. I can consider it market research, but it's more about how much I respect Sloane's opinion.

"Are you going to make fun of me?"

"Not at all," I say. "I really want to know."

"Well, besides the obvious—that Rocks is ultra-hot—I liked that it was this sweeping, romantic setting." She indicates the beach in front of her. "I'm here now, but I'm not usually, and my bedroom becomes the beach. This fabulous resort. I can escape the sleet and snow in Pittsburgh and I know that in four hundred pages, I'll have a happily-ever-after."

"Mm." My books aren't quite that long, but I get what she's saying. "And you want that happily-ever-after for yourself."

"Of course I do," she says. "Who wouldn't?"

I smile over the top of her head again, because that's a great question. I love writing romance novels, because I love providing the happily-ever-after for the people I put in danger of not getting it. They always do, and readers expect them to.

I want them to myself.

My mind spins, and my pulse sprints. I hum to try to quiet everything inside me, and say, "I have a confession."

"Another one?"

"I told you I had a few things to tell you on this trip."

"Mm."

I ignore her imitation of my humming, shake my head,

and then lower it until my mouth is very close to her ear. "I'm worried about kissing you."

She flinches, her body suddenly in a much tighter stance. "You are?"

"What if...?"

She only waits for a couple of extra beats before supplying, "It's not hot?"

I swallow, but she's nailed it. "I mean, that might be a little blunt."

"I'm always a little blunt," she says with a sigh. "I've been thinking about it too."

"You have?"

"Why wouldn't I be?"

"I don't know." The conversation stalls there, and I'm not sure how to pick it up. Switching to another topic doesn't seem like the thing to do, and as the water keeps talking and talking, we sit there silent.

I've never minded the silence with Sloane. She doesn't let a lot of it in, but when she does, it's meaningful. Behind us, the music stops. The lights start to get extinguished, and I twist to look.

"Looks like the party is over."

A couple of resort staff come to get the tiki torches from the beach area, and one says, "Sorry, the beach is closing."

"All right." Sloane gets up and reaches across her lounger for her drink. A wave comes up, and she shifts in the sand as it does. "Oh." She stumbles, and down she goes.

I hurry after her, especially when she cries out. If she goes into blood shock again I'm definitely not kissing her tonight. "Hey, are you okay?" I drop to my knees in the surf, and I'm sure I'll have sand everywhere I don't want it.

Sloane giggles and says, "I spilled my drink." She grabs my hand and pulls me all the way down to the sand.

"Yeah, you did."

The loungers get taken back up the beach, and a gentleman says, "I'm sorry, but you must come up to the building."

"Yes," I say. "We will. We're coming."

He leaves, and I get to my feet. I extend my hand to Sloane, and I help her up. In one of my books, she might've pulled the hero to the ground, and they'd roll around in the gentle waves while they make out, letting sand get into everything they don't want. Because they don't care. They're that into each other.

But I'm not living in a romance novel, and while I hope Sloane is my heroine, I still haven't figured out how to kiss her. The heroes in my books always know how to kiss their women. How, and when, and where. They always give the best kiss of their lives, and they always get it in return.

I have no idea if that will happen for us, and it makes me not want to try at all.

She gets to her feet, gives me a shy smile, and we pick

our way back up to the building. The party has dispersed, and there's not even a butler to be found.

"I have sand everywhere," she says.

"There's the outdoor shower." I nod to it as we approach. "I could use it too." I stand back and gesture to it. "You go first."

She moves past me and turns on the shower. We've used it before, and it's nice to rinse the saltwater off my skin and get the sand out of my swimming trunks so it's not all over the room.

I watch her, the light from the building shining on her, haloing her in light. If I was standing in front of her, I'd be able to see her, but on the dark side, she's even more gorgeous lit as she is.

She runs her hands through her hair as she moves under the stream of water, and I want to do that so badly. I take the couple of steps to her and slide my hand along her elbow. It's pointing straight up at the sky, and that means my fingertips tiptoe down her armpit and the side of her body.

She leans back into me, a soft sound coming out of her mouth. It's not quite the moan I'm hoping for, but she turns in my arms, her eyes searching my face. The light bathes me, and I wonder what she sees.

I don't hesitate this time. I take her fully in my arms, the shower raining down on both of us and I finally, finally kiss her.

I can admit I'm a little hesitant at first, but with one

taste of her lips, I'm starving for more, so my second stroke is twice as hard as the first, twice as eager, ten times as good.

Her fingers slide through my wet hair, and I feel sand along her shoulders as I keep kissing her. I can't get enough, and this definitely isn't like kissing my sister or my best friend.

It feels like we're standing on a ledge above a bonfire, the heat licking up my feet to my legs to my chest. It consumes me, and I'm still kissing Sloane.

I finally break contact, only to move my lips to her neck, because I have to taste her there now. Everywhere.

She utters that delicious moan I heard during her massage, and I smile against her collarbone. "There it is," I whisper.

Sloane takes my face in her hands and lifts my head, matching her mouth to mine this time—and it's in the form of a smile which I quickly kiss away.

Chapter Thirteen
Sloane

I'm nowhere near ready to fall into bed with Logan, but kissing in the shower? I had no idea that was on the radar for tonight. Or ever, until we are ready to say *I love you*, and wear diamond rings, and stand at altars.

And I don't know if I'll ever be able to do the last one. Not in the traditional sense, at least. No, there will be no long engagement, no dress fittings, no cake sampling. I loved all of that the first time, but that was Before, and this is After.

I'm not the same woman I was five years ago, and I'd like to think I'm a better, more mature version of her, so I don't need all that traditional wedding stuff to have an amazing ceremony with the man of my dreams.

I haven't kissed anyone in a long, long time, and I can't imagine going a day without this touch in my life. Kissing is so intimate, so passionate, and so vulnerable for me that I feel naked in the shower with Logan.

My best friend, and very decidedly my boyfriend. This kiss doesn't have an ounce of brotherliness in it, and for that, I am thrilled beyond measure.

He finally pulls away from this second kiss, but he doesn't go far. He doesn't step out of the shower stream and keeps brushing his hands down my shoulders. "Turn around," he whispers, and I do.

He lovingly strokes those big hands down my back and through my hair until he says, "I think I got it all."

I turn toward him again and run my hands down his wet tee. "You got any sand under this?"

He chuckles and says, "Wanna find out?"

Boy, do I ever. I nod while he peels the shirt over his head and discards it at our feet. There's enough light hitting his back to catch on the ridges of his muscles, and I slick my hands along them. "There's a little," I whisper, feeling the fine grains of sand and sweeping them away from his skin.

He says nothing, his gaze heavy on my face. I can't look at him, though. "I..."

"Nothing's changed," he says in that commanding voice. "Okay, Sloane?" He puts his hand under my chin and lifts it, forcing me to look at him. "I know you're not ready for more than what just happened. I'm fine with it."

"We're sharing that room," I say, hating how tinny my voice is. "That big bed..." I sigh and bend to turn over my sandal so I can step into it. I hadn't even realized I'd lost a shoe; the kiss was that good.

"Nothing's changed," he says.

"Yes, Logan, something's changed." I look at him, the soft glow from the nearby building lights hitting both of us. I don't want to be upset about the kissing or the fact that I'm not ready to do more than that. It's just the first step, and that thought calms me.

"That was an amazing kiss." I cradle his face in one hand while the water from the shower still hits his back. "What did you think?"

"Phenomenal," he whispers, and somehow, that one word makes me feel like his most prized possession.

Neither one of us has a towel, but we step out of the shower and Logan turns it off. A butler emerges from the stone arch once we've gone up the few steps to the courtyard, and he hands us both a towel.

"Thank you," Logan murmurs for both of us, and he dries off as we continue toward the elevator. I really need two towels—one for my body and one to contain my hair, so I focus there. If I can get that to stop dripping, my swimming suit dries quickly.

He takes a couple of minutes in the bathroom to get changed, and then he turns it over to me to shower. I'd been planning on it anyway, as I need to wash away the sunscreen, the lotions, the salt, and the day every evening.

Logan breathes evenly when I return to the room, fully pajamaed and ready to sleep for a long, long time.

Only my lamp remains on, and it's clear he was ready for bed and took the opportunity to get some shut eye before I came out and started talking to him again.

We've had a couple of days of more relaxing activities here at the resort, but tomorrow, we're leaving the property again. This time for an afternoon of ziplining through the jungle.

Right now, I don't want to go, but I know it'll be something Logan will love, and I want him to have fun on this vacation too. Thankfully, we don't have to meet our tour guide until noon, and that means I can set my alarm for later in the morning.

Fat chance I'll actually be able to sleep past six or seven. I'm up early at home, and I've only slept in a couple of times here. Logan is always up before me, usually doing something on his computer or reading on the balcony.

I close my eyes and breathe in deeply. For every inhale and exhale, I count. *One...two...three.* This settles my mind and my pulse to the point that I can truly hope every woman on the planet can have an outdoor shower kiss with the man of their dreams.

Then I blank when I think of Logan that way. I've loved him for a long time, but in a different way than how men and women love each other when they're dating and getting married.

To distract myself from going too far down this track, I look at my phone and check my email. I've had to manage a few things while I've been gone, but Lucy has done a great job keeping things going for me. Another woman at my real estate firm has handled anything that Lucy can't, and I see a couple of things from my assistant, as well as Peyton.

I tap out answers with my thumbs and get those emails sent for tomorrow. I ignore the messages coming in from the form and quickly forward them along to Lucy. She should've gotten them anyway, but she hasn't answered either. I'd know, because I'd have gotten her reply too.

With work handled for another day, I plug in my device and thumb through the texts from my mom and sisters. For some reason, I haven't answered any of them yet. My time to do so is running out, but I don't feel up to it. I stand up. Lamp off; blanket pulled down; alarm set for later in the morning.

I'm finally ready for bed, and I slip between the sheets. Logan's breathing hitches, and I roll toward him and adjust my pillows so they're where I want them.

"Sloane," he murmurs in his sleep, reaching for me.

I pull my pillow toward him and move that way. He cradles me against his chest, and I take a deep breath of his skin. He's salty and musky, the scent of his cologne like a permanent friend I don't think even the ocean can wash off.

He once again reminds me of home, and we both fall asleep in only two breaths.

* * *

"I am not stepping off of this," I say the next afternoon.

"You can do it." Logan's presence behind me doesn't give me the courage I hope it will.

"It's like a hundred feet down." I look down, which is a *huge* mistake. Huge. My stomach swoops, and there is *no way* I'm stepping off this platform.

"It's only thirty-five," he says, the smile in his voice. I wouldn't know, because I'm still staring at the spot on the ground where I'm going to die.

"Not helping."

"You're strapped in." His hand comes down on my hip. "And no pressure, but there's six of us up here, and you're up first."

"Logan." My voice trembles. "I can't."

"You absolutely can," he says, that powerful voice telling me he'd never lie to me. Of course he wouldn't. Logan knows how important it is for me to have absolute honesty between me and the people in my life. I wouldn't have gotten all the way to the altar without a groom if Leon had been honest with me.

"It's one step, Sloane," he says next. "You're all set. Strapped in. You're going to love it. It's like flying."

"I hate you," I whimper.

He says nothing, and I look at the man who'd helped get all the straps in place around my legs and hips. He wears a bored expression, but I can feel the impatience of the people seething behind me.

"Fine." I step away from Logan and toward the worker.

"You're going to love it," Logan says again. "Scream all you want."

I don't have the wherewithal to give him a withering look over my shoulder. I'm so focused on the man in front of me. He clips me to the line and shows me again where to put my hands. "Sit down," he says, mimicking what I'm supposed to do by bending his knees as if he's sitting down into a chair.

"If I die..." I say over my shoulder.

"I'll call your mom," Logan says, oh-so-helpfully.

"No." I face him. "Not my mom. *Rose.* You have to call Rose first."

He grins like he's really enjoying this conversation about my death. "You're not going to die."

"We'll see." I face the jungle again and follow the line through the trees. Surely there's been people as heavy as me on this thing. They had a harness that fit me, and it wasn't even the largest one.

I take a deep breath, shuffle to the very edge of the platform, and close my eyes. My heartbeat pounds through my ears and head, but I tell myself I can do this. Logan and I have transitioned our friendship into something more, and kissing him is life-changing every time it happens.

Feeling brave and strong, I sit down and find myself flying through the jungles of Belize. I do scream for the first couple of seconds, because it's *scary* to be up this high with nothing beneath my feet. After that, though, it's simply amazing.

Amazing to be this free. Amazing to feel the air rushing around me, the green of the leaves flashing beside me I'm moving so fast. Amazing to feel the way birds do, like I'm flying and nothing will ever catch me.

The man at the next platform catches me, of course, and I'm very grateful he does. I only have a couple of minutes to get off this line and platform, because the rest of the tour guests will be coming behind me. Starting with Logan.

I stand still, my breath laboring through my lungs, as I get unclipped. I've gone up the two flights of stairs toward the next launch pad before I hear Logan coming. He whoops and pumps his fist, which simply makes joy explode through me.

He lands on the platform and runs a couple of steps before easing to a graceful stop. I'd stopped, but I'd very nearly fallen flat on my face in the process.

"How was it?" he calls up to me while he gets unclipped.

"Great," I call down to him. He comes bounding up the stairs, and since there's still one person in front of me before I can be clipped to the next line, he wraps me up in his arms.

"Just great?" he asks.

"Amazing." I laugh with him. "Really amazing." I look

up at him, at the happy crinkles resting in the corners of his eyes, at those straight, white teeth, at his own joy.

We move toward each other at the same time, and there will never be anything as great, amazing, or phenomenal as kissing Logan Murphy in the jungle.

* * *

I moan as I sink into the hot water. I've sat in the jacuzzi on our balcony before, but Logan wouldn't get in with me. Tonight, he's only one step behind me, and the water sloshes around me as his body sinks into the water too.

He sighs too, and our eyes meet. "One of the best days of my life," I say.

"Yeah?"

I nod, and he says, "I'm glad, Sloane."

I've noticed that since we've broken down the friend zone and stepped out of it, neither of us have been using our nicknames much. He calls me Sloane and not Sloany, and I only use Murph when I'm trying to get him to relax and party up a little bit.

I slide over and sit immediately beside him. "Where should we go next year?"

"You're already thinking ahead to next year?"

"We usually do."

"Yeah." Logan falls quiet, and I don't like it.

"What?"

"Do you think we'll keep doing our mid-winter trip?" he asks. "If I move to Pittsburgh?"

"*If?*" I don't mean to screech the word, but I sort of do. "I thought you *were* moving to Pittsburgh."

"I haven't decided one-hundred percent yet," he says, keeping his voice low to match the night. It's a low-energy night, with the sun down already and the roar of the ocean in the background. We had an amazing afternoon of ziplining, and then a low-key dinner at the Japanese restaurant here at the resort.

I bat at a rose petal as it floats toward me. "What's influencing your decision?"

"Kissing you."

"That went well," I point out.

"My parents."

I nod and skim my hands along the water's surface in front of me. "You haven't told them anything yet."

"I have not."

"Your mom will love me," I say as I look at him. I need him to say *of course she will,* because apparently, I'm that needy.

He grins at me. "I'm sure she will." His arm comes around me, and I lean into his side.

"I could come to Superior."

"You would suffocate in Superior, sweetheart." He touches a kiss to my temple. "There's no way I'd ask you to move there."

"It would get me away from my mom."

"Did you text her back yet?"

I shake my head. There's so much that goes into my day, from managing several dozen moving pieces of buying and selling real estate in the city, to answering personal texts, to dreaming about owning a dog, to how I'm going to feed myself for another day.

Both of my sisters and my mom have texted me in the past couple of days, and I haven't found the energy to respond to any of them. I should, because my mother will call the United States embassy here in Belize if I don't, and I'm not even kidding.

Rose will know something major has happened, and she'll demand to know what without even saying hello once she gets me on the phone. Kenna will just be annoyed I haven't validated her frustration with her professor. I should be sure to text them all tonight before bed to avoid the bulk of the drama.

"Why not?" he asks.

"I don't want to share you with anyone yet," I whisper.

"You'll tell your mom?"

"I'll have to," I say. "She's always thought we were hooking up on these trips as it is. She asks way more questions about you after the mid-winter trip."

"Does she?" He kneads me closer. "That's...interesting."

"She'll be hurt," I say. "She's still in a delicate place with everything going on with my dad."

"I know." Logan touches his mouth lower on my neck,

and I turn into him to kiss him properly. This kiss accelerates quickly, and he lifts me onto his lap a moment later. He groans, and I think it's because of my weight and try to slip away.

"Stop it," he growls, holding me in place.

"I'm crushing you."

"Not even close." He kisses me again, and it's been so long since anyone has looked at me the way he does. Since anyone has wanted to kiss me the way he is.

I moan into his mouth, not even trying to make the noise I know he likes. It just happens. I want to whisper something sexy as he drops his mouth to my throat, but nothing comes to mind. Nothing I want to say to my best friend, at least.

I'm wearing a one-piece tonight, but it has thin straps over my shoulders and triangles for the bust, despite my breasts being very, very round. The V-neck goes all the way to my navel, and it's high-cut on my thighs too.

His fingers brush my sides, and I twist around so I'm straddling him instead of sitting on his lap.

Logan breathes in hard, and I love the sound of it. Still, terror streams through me, because this is my best friend. The man who rescued me in Mexico five years ago, and the same one who's booked our mid-winter trip every year since.

South Carolina, Oahu, Grand Cayman, and St. Lucia. This year, we'd decided to stay domestic again and go to Florida, until that flood landed us here.

Here.

Is this where I want to be?

Warring emotions split my attention, part of me screaming *yes! Yes, this is where we want to be!* while another, hissing, slithering part of me tells me not to ruin the only good relationship in my life with...well, me.

His eyes meet mine, and he's breathing normally as he says, "Where are you?"

"My knees hurt," I say, slipping away from him. It's a hot tub on a balcony, so I don't have much wiggle room. Even if I cross to the other side, my legs would be all tangled with his in a matter of seconds.

I'm sweating from the amazing kissing, and that's only amplified by the hot water lapping against my stomach. Terrified out of my mind, but absolutely loving the way he looks at my body—at me; right at me—I can't meet his gaze.

"I think this hot tub is too hot." I lift myself out of it and sit on the edge, not wanting to kiss him so completely and then run.

"You could go shower," he says. "I'll stay out here." He sounds casual, and I don't detect any measure of forced-ness behind it. All at once, a thought hits me like a metal baseball bat knocking a home run out of the park.

This is a fling. A mid-winter fling in a summery place.

I stand and walk away, actually hoping he's not looking. Of course he is. I feel the weight of those eyes on my backside as I grab a towel and hurry to wrap it around myself. Inside, I suck in a breath as I slide the door closed. I have half a mind to lock it, but I don't.

Logan isn't going to come creeping into the bathroom while I'm in there. He'll let me talk to the water and let it wash down the drain, and I force the idea of this being a fling for him—for either of us—into the pipes where it belongs.

I promise myself I won't revisit it again until my irrational hour, and I whisper to the sudsy water as it flows down my body. "This is not a fling for me."

I can only hope and pray it's not for Logan either.

Chapter Fourteen
Sloane

"How dare he?" I say when Kenna answers the phone. Logan's off running somewhere at the resort, and then he'll shower in preparation for our shopping day. There are two ships in port today, and we've decided that's the best time to head to the more touristy area of Belize and get a few souvenirs for our friends and family.

"He gave you a C on that paper? The one you had the tutor go over for you?"

"Yes," Kenna chirps back at me. She's twenty-two and in her senior year at Dartmouth. "A C!"

"Do you want me to email him?" I totally act like I will, though we both know I won't. Kenna will never let me anyway.

"No," she says in resignation. "And...the tutor didn't really go over it as thoroughly as he probably could've."

She clears her throat, and that's the equivalent to Logan's throat-humming. She's saying something without saying it, and I narrow my eyes out at the ocean. The view from my balcony is so stunning, with shades of blue, teal, turquoise, and green I've never seen before. The wind blows ashore harder this morning than other days, but I don't mind it. It's strong enough to push my thick hair off my face, and I get a little relief from the weight of it all.

"Kenna," I say in a warning tone. "Explain that."

"He's really cute," she says. "No, handsome. You're always telling me to find a *handsome* man, Sloane. And—" She hits the D hard. "He's handsome. And a good kisser."

I grin to the waves. "So you paid him to read your essay—oh, I mean, kiss you while he's at work."

"He did both," she says in a high-pitched tone. "Sort of."

I laugh, and that gives Kenna permission to do so as well. "Plus, he asked me out afterward, and we're semi-dating now."

I sober, maybe a little too quickly. "But you're not going to marry him, Ken. You're twenty-two."

"I'm aware."

I don't know why I'm so protective of my sisters. I don't want them to go through the same heartache I had to, or anything like what our mother is dealing with. "What's his name?" I ask.

"I don't want to say."

"It's Ethan, isn't it? You know you can't even *speak* to

an Ethan." I've known quite a few Ethan's in my life, and they're all rowdy frat boys with loud laughs, bellies that will bulge by the time they hit thirty from how much beer they drink, and-or behavior problems.

"It's not Ethan, calm down."

"I'm perfectly calm."

"It's Chad."

"Okay..." I pause, trying to find the words. A smile curves my lips. "That might actually be worse." I giggle, but Kenna belly-laughs.

"Right?" She sighs. "Anyway, how's Belize? Magical?"

"Tropical," I say. "I'm currently standing on my balcony and watching the waves come ashore. It's supposed to be eighty-four degrees today."

"I hate you."

I laugh again while she says it's been snowing on and off for two days in Pennsylvania. "You just need a mid-winter trip," I tell her.

"Yeah, well, we don't all have someone like Logan," she says.

I fall silent again, which isn't a good thing. Kenna isn't Rose, but she can pick up pieces when they're as big as the one I just put down. I hear her intake of breath, and I cut her off before she can ask.

"Oh, we're off," I say brightly. Fakely. "He's here. Talk later, Ken."

"Sloany," she screeches, and I pause in my attempt to hang up on her.

"What?" I ask, a hint of impatience in my voice. I really don't want to talk about Logan. Not with Kenna. Not with Rose. Not with my mom. I'd spoken true when I'd told him last night I wanted to keep him to myself. It's obvious Kenna has seen something special between us previously, and I want to ask her what it is. How she saw it. Why didn't I?

"Have fun for me," Kenna says. "Come home safe."

"I will," I say. "Now, go fix that paper—and this time, hire a really ugly tutor to help you go over it." We laugh again, and the call ends without me running with my tail tucked between my legs.

Instead of calling Rose, I text her. *Having so much fun! Sorry I didn't call. There's not great service here at the resort, and I've been in and out of cenotes, the jungle, and the ocean. Lunch when I get back?*

That will appease her until I land in Pittsburgh on Sunday evening, and already I feel the weight of my real life descending on me. We have three more days here. Today, tomorrow, and Saturday. We travel all day Sunday, with another monster layover in Atlanta before we have to separate to fly to our respective cities.

I've never wanted my mid-winter trip to continue as badly as I do this year. I like the bubble Logan and I have created for ourselves here, and I love answering a few emails and calling that my day's work before eating really good food, squeezing myself into another sexy swimming suit, and kissing Logan like this isn't a fling at all.

Maybe if I kiss him with enough passion, if he's thinking fling, he'll change his mind. He kisses me like his life depends on having his mouth on mine, and that doesn't read fling to me. But I've read men and situations wrong before. Very, very wrong.

"I'm jumping in the shower," Logan says behind me, startling me. I spin toward him, my phone up and ready to throw with all my might. He sees me, and I'm not sure what shows on my face, but his dissolves into amusement and surprise at the same time.

"Are you going to throw that pearly pink phone at me?"

"If necessary." I lower it, the adrenaline pumping through me slowing enough now that I know he's not a threat.

He laughs as he bowls into me, wrapping me up in his arms and legs as I stumble backward. "Logan," I chastise. "The railing is right there."

"Oh, you're not going to fall." He steadies me and those intensely blue eyes gaze into mine. "I've got you." He leans down and kisses me, and while it starts out sweet and slow, we both quickly accelerate it to something more.

I want to kiss him forever, and I want to stay in this room forever, and I want to live in Belize for forever.

He rests his forehead against mine, and I keep my eyes closed as I ask, "Do we have to go home?"

"Mm." That one means, *Yes, Sloane. We have to go home.* He's been working in the mornings, I know, though he hasn't told me as much. He's up before me, and he always closes his computer the moment I make any noise whatsoever.

"Maybe we can just find a little apartment here."

A chuckle this time. That means, *We aren't moving here, Sloane.*

I open my eyes and look up at him. "This is real, right?"

He blinks, shock registering in those dazzling eyes for a moment. Another blink: hurt. Another: anger. He steps away from me. "You think I'm...what, exactly, Sloane?"

Oh, I don't like it when he says my name like that. The single syllable slaps me, and I press back into the railing. "It's just...in my irrational hour, I had this thought like maybe this was a fling."

I turn and face the ocean. "I know it's stupid. It's probably just me, because this is new, and..." I wait as he steps beside me, because my voice isn't going to be able to over-power the wind. "Scary."

He says nothing for probably a full minute. "What's your irrational hour?" he asks.

I glance over to him. "That's what you got out of what I said?"

"The thought started there," he says. "I need to under-stand it."

"It's this hour in the middle of the night. Early morn-ing." I wave into the wind, indicating the enormity of the ocean. "I have to get up to go to the bathroom, so I'm awake, and in the time after I go back to bed and when I fall asleep again, I have all these irrational thoughts."

"So you know they're irrational."

"They're loud in the middle of the night."

"Or early morning." He nudges me with his elbow, clearly teasing me. "It lasts a whole hour?"

"The time when it happens doesn't matter," I snap at him. "Nor does how long it actually lasts. This is *real*, Logan. I'm freaking out."

"I can see that." He sighs and turns his back on the ocean. After running his hands through his hair, which has only gotten longer in the past week, he dares to peek at me. "This is new and scary," he acknowledges.

I appreciate that so, so much. I don't even realize how much until my eyes burn with tears. I press them closed and seize onto the heat there. Hopefully the wind will dry them before they can fall, before Logan notices them. "It's so bright out here," I say, but my nasally voice gives me away.

"This is not a fling." He must need a few moments of silence to summon that power in his voice, because he wasn't speaking like that until this sentence. I at once feel reassured and safe with him, and I nod.

"For me," he adds. "Is it for you?"

I snap my eyes open and nearly get blinded, first by the sun and then by the sharpness in his eyes. "No." I shake my head. "Absolutely not."

He bobs his head too, something burning in those eyes

he doesn't want me to see. His eyes fall almost closed as he drops his chin, then he steps past me, his hand lingering on my shoulder. "I'm going to go shower then."

Logan leaves me to my idiotic thoughts, the whipping wind, and the sound of the ocean. My phone chimes, and it's the *snapple-beep* I've assigned to Lucy. She's only texted me a handful of times in the past week, so it has to be important. Logan will be another twenty minutes at least, and I return to the room only to grab my laptop so I can get a few things done at work while I wait.

Work.

The thought of returning to snowy Pittsburgh and stepping into a pencil skirt and a pair of heels in only a few days has my heart plummeting toward my ankles. It falls fast too, because I've always loved my job. Showing houses gives me life. Staging a space for the photographer is like oxygen to me. Writing up listings is like putting the can opener on a huge can of Dreams and starting to open it for someone.

If I don't have my job, I literally have nothing.

"Logan," I whisper. I've always had Logan, and just because we're kissing and holding hands and talking about the future only means he'll still be in my life.

A tremor of fear moves through my belly, because Logan doesn't know the real me. He only knows After Work Sloane, as she complains about the twelve hours she's put in that day while her microwavable lasagna rotates behind her. He knows Mid-Winter Trip Sloane, who barely works, always has a cute swimming suit and a quick jab at something he's said.

But he doesn't know *me*, and the thought of him coming to Pittsburgh and learning who I really am, what life with me would really be like, has a fresh set of tears pressing behind my eyelids.

If that happens, he won't like what he sees. I have to figure out how to convince him to stay in Superior. We can long-distance date. I can fly up there every other weekend, and he can come visit me for major holidays.

I shake my head and tell myself, "You're not kids of divorced parents, going back and forth." Then I focus on my email, determined not to worry about unknown future scenarios between me and Logan.

That's simply what my brain does, and I'm so relieved when Logan pokes his head out onto the balcony and says, "Ready, sweetheart?"

I snap the laptop closed. "Yes." There's nothing as mind-numbing and therapeutic for me as shopping, and I am so ready to shop this day to death. Maybe my thoughts will follow.

Chapter Fifteen
Logan

"Mm, you are the flavor I've been missing in my life." I stir my mocha caramel milkshake and grin at it appreciatively. It's creamy, with the perfect amount of coffee flavoring and the caramel not that fake kind that leaves a film on my tongue.

"Wish you'd said that to me," Sloane says dryly, cocking her eyebrows at me.

I look at her, trying to figure out what she wants from me in this moment. We've been shopping all day long, and I feel like I patiently went into each and every store she wanted to, browsed through things I have zero interest in, and exclaimed appropriately over the souvenirs she picked out for her boss, her assistant, both of her sisters, and her mom and dad.

I bought a couple of things—a magnet in the shape of the country of Belize for myself and a tea towel with a heart over the capital city for my mother. I don't have close friends outside of Sloane, nor co-workers I'd be buying gifts for. If Sloane noticed how little I bought, she hasn't commented on it.

I reach over and cover Sloane's hand. "You are the flavor I've been missing in my life."

She puts another bite of her chocolate brownie bite shake in her mouth. "What flavor is that?"

"Chocolate," I say, leaning toward her. "Chocolate would go great with my mocha caramel." I touch my lips to hers, and she lets me. She doesn't truly kiss me, and I'm not sure what I've done wrong.

She was contemplative on the balcony this morning, but we talked through her "irrational hour" thoughts. We had a great lunch in the shops, and I've been holding her hand, laughing with her, and generally enjoying the day with her.

"Are you okay?" I ask.

"Fine." She gazes past me to the water, and I know she's not fine. She'll tell the ocean and the shower her secrets, but she won't divulge them to me until she's ready.

Impatience tugs at my heartstrings, and I instantly pull back. I've waited a long time to be with Sloane Sanders the way we are now, and I can be patient for more. In all, she's taken everything I've told her in stride. For someone who dislikes changes as much as she does, I actually think she's transitioned to the idea of us romantically quite well.

I don't know what else to say, so I remain quiet. Sloane

will come back to me in a few minutes, or I'll draw her back by asking her something. I feel the end of our vacation looming over me, over us, and I dislike it greatly.

I want to push against the pressure ballooning around us and keep it at bay. Keep us insulated from the drudgery of everyday life.

"What's your favorite thing to eat for lunch?" I ask.

Sloane blinks, slowly coming back to me. "There's this great butcher block and deli on Forrest Street in Pittsburgh," she says. "They have this grilled sirloin sandwich..." Her voice trails off and then she smacks her lips. "It's phenomenal."

Phenomenal.

That's how I described kissing her, and it's one-hundred percent true. "Sounds amazing," I press out of my narrow throat. "I think we have to get back to the golf cart depository." I stand and swirl my spoon through the remainder of my shake. I don't want it anymore if I can't have a taste of her chocolate with it, and I turn to toss it in the trashcan.

When I face her again, she's on her feet too, extending her half-empty cup to me. I take it, but don't move after that. "I want us to be okay."

She softens. "We are okay."

"You don't seem okay."

"I'm thinking a lot today."

"I hate it when you think."

"Gee, thanks, Murph."

I note the use of my nickname and turn away from her before she can see anything in my eyes. I honestly can't classify what's streaming through me. Worry? Fear?

Love...

"I just mean." I turn back to her. "Sometimes you go into the deep end with your thoughts. They take on a life of their own, and they're not..."

"Real," we say together. I reach for her hand to ground her. "This," I say emphatically. "This is what's real. I'm here, and I *want* to be here. Right *here*. This *is* real."

She nods, her pretty blue eyes filling with tears. "I'm sorry, Logan." She crashes into my arms, and I simply hold her on this grimy deck outside an ice cream shop while she cries into my chest. I don't know what to say to comfort her, so I simply stroke her hair and stand strong amidst the storm raging through her.

I wave off a couple of waitstaff until Sloane's composed herself enough to pull away. I don't say anything while she uses the hem of her tee to wipe her eyes. She won't look at me, but she takes my hand and leads me away from our table and off the deck. I go with her, because I'm fairly certain I just fell in love with her standing on that hot deck, the scent of garbage rising on the breeze and her sobbing into my shoulder.

We walk down the sidewalk to the road, where we move in front of a couple of elderly people almost on top of us. We're way faster than them, and I gently lead Sloane back toward the bus stop. We'll get a taxi there back to the golf cart station, and that'll take us back to our resort.

"What do you dream about?" she asks me as we cross a street, the Central American sun beating down on our shoulders.

"Mm." That's my indication that I need a few minutes to think about this question. I don't answer it while we wait for the taxi, and she doesn't ask again. When we finally get settled in a car for the first leg of our trip back to the resort, I squeeze her hand and say, "I dream of warm weather."

"That so doesn't count."

"You didn't let me finish."

She gestures to tell me to continue.

"I dream of warm weather where I can sit outside and write." I swallow. "Every day. Where I don't have to use a whisk to get the snow out of Titan's fur, where there's not these horrible months where things are frozen in the morning and melted in the afternoon, so you don't know if you need boots or just slippers to go get your mail."

Sloane looks at me, and I finally swing my attention to her. "What?"

"*That's* what you dream about? Warm weather?"

I run my hand through my hair. "I've got to get out of Wisconsin."

"Pittsburgh has all the things you just listed."

"So let's go to Florida," I say, a certain desperation

clawing up my throat. I can feel the talons against my vocal cords, shredding them, and I try to clear it all away.

"Did you just clear your throat? Like, legit, clearing of the throat?"

I roll my eyes. "Stop it."

"I'm not moving to Florida," she says.

"Texas then," I say. "It's warm there year-round." I look at her with hope marching through me, though I don't believe for a single second either of us will move to Texas, Florida, or anywhere else.

She shakes her head, a small smile spreading her lips. It's faint and doesn't last long, but it feels like it's shining with the power of the sun to me.

"What do you dream about?" I ask.

"Mm."

"Come on," I say. "I told you."

"I'd like to have someone in my house when I come home after work."

"Like, a stalker?"

She elbows me. "No." Her eyes catch mine, and everything sobers between us. Time stretches, and I lean over and wait for her to close the last inch between us. Our breath mingles, and Sloane's eyes drift closed.

"I want a companion. A husband who adores me and orders my favorite thing for dinner when I lose a sale—before he even knows I've lost the sale. Someone who can take care of our dog and will vacuum the Cheetos crumbs out of my SUV."

Her lips catch on mine a couple of times, but neither one of us perpetuates the kiss.

"I want to know that if I fall in love again, it'll last. That I won't end up like my mom, with secrets and lies and betrayal once again weighing me down."

She wants perfection, and I want to give it to her. "Not to be a downer or anything, but..." I whisper. "That sounds impossible."

"That's what a dream is, Logan. It's impossible." She lowers her head and leans it against my shoulder, the moment to kiss her gone and over. We settle into silence that lasts all the way back to our room, where Sloane packs her souvenirs into her suitcase before gathering everything she needs for a shower.

"You're getting in early tonight," I say. "Should I plan on room service?"

"Sure," she says, her voice full of pep but her face broadcasting sadness. Everything falls as she goes past me, and I really want to do something about it. I want to promise her impossible dreams. I'll throw a rope and harness the moon, pull it as close as she wants it.

But even I can't do that. I can write a happily-ever-after from start to finish, but life inside novels is rarely as messy as a single day a real human being lives. We try to capture the emotions, the super high highs, and the horrible lows—and everything in between—but it's hard to do with only words.

We don't get pictures, and we can't describe every

human emotion as it passes across someone's face. Sometimes I can't even separate the many and varied emotions I'm experiencing at one time, and I'm not a female.

"She's confused," I mutter to myself as I pick up the remote and navigate to the room service menu. Of course she's confused; she started seeing me through romantic eyes a week ago. One week.

I've been crushing on her—hard—for years. I've had plenty of nights to think about how a relationship between us would—or wouldn't—work. My heartbeat skips over itself as I think about how I felt about her this evening over milkshakes.

I have no reasons why Sloane and I won't work. Every scenario, every single thing I can think of, goes away, because I'll do whatever she wants. I'll live where she wants, in the house she wants. I'll order the dinners she wants, and I'll run with the dogs—all of whom will love her more than me—and I'll vacuum her SUV every weekend.

Because she's my home, and I just need to find a way to get her to see it. I start with pork nachos, chips and guac, and cheesecake with a berry assortment. Then I add on a key lime pie and a couple of bottles of Belizean beer, because I still have one more thing to tell Sloane before we leave this country, and I need a little alcohol to help get my tongue loose.

Chapter Sixteen
Sloane

"Who keeps calling you?" I look over as Logan's phone goes off again. It's resting on his chest, and he doesn't even move to look at it. His eyes remain steadfastly closed, in fact.

We've eaten ourselves into double comas, and still, I reach for another swipe of my finger through the rich, delicious, tart berry sauce on the plate that brought cheesecake with it.

Logan snores softly, and I dare to reach over to him. Taking precious seconds to really determine if he's asleep or not, I decide he is. By then, the call has gone to voicemail, but I still lift his phone gently from his chest.

He's missed four calls from someone named Alicia. No last name. I tap to see more, but he's got a passcode on his device, and I don't know it. I can probably guess at the four-digit PIN, but I'm not going to invade his privacy like that. Just the fact that I've seen Alicia call four times—oh, five, as his phone starts ringing again—makes me feel slimy.

I have half a mind to answer it and take a message, just to get her to stop. But I don't know who she is; Logan has never mentioned anyone named Alicia in our chats or calls. So I press the volume button on the side of his phone to turn it down so I don't have to hear it go off the next time she calls, and gently lower the phone back to his chest.

He turns his head but doesn't wake, and I quickly swipe my finger through the berry sauce again. I love room service with my whole heart, and thankfully, we have an equivalent in Pittsburgh: Diner Delivery. I can order anything with the app, and a half-hour later, I'm eating as if I've cooked a feast.

It doesn't do anything for the dream I spilled to Logan earlier tonight, about wanting someone to come home to at night. I'd love to see his face every day after work, but I'm worried he won't be as thrilled to see mine.

And I need him to be. I look over to him and study the gentle stubble along his jaw. It forms a perfect beard that's soft, even after only a week, and I wonder which of my insecurities and flaws I need to tamp down first in order to keep him in my life.

On the surface, Logan and I make perfect sense. I'm sensible and put-together. He's employed, yet sponta-neous. I could stand to loosen up my schedule a little bit, especially on the weekends, and I wouldn't be irritated with him for mooching off me like some of my previous boyfriends.

I want to believe every word out of Logan's mouth, as I always have. But something has been knocked loose by my father in recent months. I've known him for my whole life, and when I look into his eyes, I don't recognize him. I never want that to be me and Murph. Ever, ever, ever.

He said my dream was impossible, and maybe he's right. I still want it, and I can't help thinking I want it with him.

"You still awake?" he mutters, and I lift the dessert plate and put it on my nightstand. That frees up the middle of the bed for sleeping, and I snap off my lamp and curl into him without brushing my teeth.

He's solid and warm and real—*this is real*, he told me earlier—and selfishly, I take my deep breath of him, hold it, and blow it out to relax. I do this a few times as he wraps me up, brings me closer, and then on the fifth breath, he whispers, "Calm enough now?"

"You missed a lot of calls," I murmur.

"Nothing important, I'm sure." His lips track their way along the side of my neck, creating a new sensation between us. He's kissed me in bed before, but usually quick, on the lips, one and done.

This is what lovers do, and immediately, my body tenses from the bottoms of my feet to a tightness in my forehead.

"Shh," he whispers, his mouth covering mine a moment later. He kisses me gently and refuses to deepen it when I try. "I don't like where you went tonight." His voice is barely in the room with us, like the wisp of smoke you can only smell, never see. "Seems like your irrational hour bled into daytime."

"Maybe," I whisper. I don't want to tell him that yes, I have to fight my thoughts all the time. Day and night. I've told him a lot about my mom and dad's situation, only holding back the things my mom has specifically asked me not to share.

They mostly speak to her insanity, and I keep her secrets, because I fear I have the same issues she does.

Of course, I tell myself. If I'd been in a loveless marriage for thirty-three years, I'd be doubting myself and everything in my life too. "She feels invisible," I say next, and Murph pulls away.

"Who? You?"

"My mom."

"I didn't realize we were talking about her."

I tuck myself under his chin, so I don't have to look at him. "I know how she feels. Sometimes I feel completely invisible too." No one really looks at that perfectly put-together and professional picture in the oval on a real estate listing. They care more about how many square feet a house has, how many bathrooms, what does the backyard look like, than they do about the person who can fill out all their complicated forms, has the market memorized so they don't have to, and works for an hour every single morning to look as good as I do.

Sometimes I wonder what it's all for. To get up and do again the next day?

"There has to be more," I say to Logan.

"I see you, sweetheart," he says. "And more to what?"

"To life."

He doesn't say anything to that, because how can he? I'm only giving him pieces of what's inside my head, and thankfully, Logan doesn't press me or ask for more information. He just holds me until I fall asleep.

The following morning, I wake to an alarm. I groan as I slap around on the nightstand to find my phone. We have two more days in Belize, and we've been to the beach; we've done snorkeling, swimming, and sunbathing. We've been through the jungles—twice. We've been shopping, done classes here at the resort, and eaten everything on the room service menu.

The day-trip to see the enormous flock of flamingos only runs every so often, and we've missed it. I told Murph we need to come back when we can see the sea of pink and watch hordes of them walk on their backward legs. He agreed.

I've always loved our ten-day trips, and this one is no different. I think I'm just ready to get back to real life, to that next step Logan and I need to take to see if we can still be Murph and Sloane, or if we'll crash and burn in these new skins of ours.

"Hiking today," I groan out, but Logan doesn't answer in his annoyingly chipper morning-person voice. We'd agreed to do one thing the other really loves today, and then spend tomorrow relaxing, eating, and packing, and that means I'm going to be hiking 1.3 miles to a waterfall and back. He's going to sit by the sea and tell me stories in his sexy, sultry voice.

I groan again, louder just for him, as I sit up. Still no response. He's usually coming out of the bathroom when my alarm goes off or working on his computer at the table or the double-wide lounger in the sitting area.

He never opens the drapes until I'm ready to get up, a fact I've noted and appreciated but not vocalized. Today, the curtains fall a little askew, like they've been caught between the jaws of the slider as it opened and then got closed, catching their threads in the track.

I get up and pull on a pair of biker shorts that go halfway down my thighs, my eyes glued to the sliding glass door in case Logan comes back inside suddenly. In the bathroom, I brush my teeth and pull on a sports bra, note the room door is still locked from the inside, and rummage through my drawer of clean things to find a tank top I haven't worn yet.

No luck there, and I pull on a bright blue one that will hopefully help the search and rescue team find my broken body if I fall to my death on our hike today. Logan must've forgotten to set his alarm, because he's the one who's kept us on schedule for our excursions on this trip.

All our trips, actually. Logan handles the details on *all* of our trips, and we still haven't chosen next year's destination. We always have it before the mid-winter trip ends, and I slide open the door and start to fight with the curtains which have immediately been sucked outside to find my way through them.

Logan says, "That's great, Alicia, thank you so much... Yes, send the paperwork over. I'm home on Sunday, and I'll have it signed by Monday morning."

I emerge onto the balcony just as Logan turns toward me. He's instantly guarded, though his voice had just held a great deal of vibrancy. When he was talking to Alicia.

"Good news?" I lift my chin, almost daring him to lie to me.

He nods, and then the party explodes onto his face. He yells as he swoops me into his arms, causing me to cry out too. "Okay," I say, shrieking as the world spins. "Okay, big fella."

He puts me down and says, "I've had to go to the bathroom for ages. Give me two minutes, and I'll come tell you everything, okay?" He doesn't wait for me to confirm. He muscles his way past the still-flying curtains and goes inside. He slams the door closed, some pieces of the drapes now stuck painfully in it.

I move to fix them when his phone rings again. He's

left it out here, and a quick glance tells me it's Alicia. He's going to tell me everything anyway...

Without thinking too hard about it, I pick up the phone and answer it with, "Logan Murphy's phone. Can I help you?"

"Oh," a woman says. "Yeah." She laughs a little, and I can't tell if it's flirty or not. "Can I really leave a message with you for Logan?"

"Of course," I say. "He's just... He just stepped out for a moment. I can have him call you right back?"

"No," she says. "I know he's roaming. Just tell him that Heartfelt Desires has approved his release date for *Beachfront Property*. June first, just like he requested."

"Release date for *Beachfront Property*," I say, drawing out the words like I'm writing them down as I do. "June first. This is for..."

"They want him to do a release day party for the book, which I know is his sticking point. You know what? Why don't you have him call me if he gets a minute?"

"Will do," ghosts out of my mouth and chatty Alicia laughs again as she ends the call.

Release day party for the book. Beachfront Property.

I practically throw his phone back onto the built-in bench seat where he'd left it, and then I yank out my device. I can do an Internet search of three words—*book Beachfront Property*—in less time than it takes to do one inhale-exhale cycle, and I'm staring at a beachy cover to a romance novel with the name L.M. Ryan on it within ten seconds.

My heart pounds beneath my breastbone in a way I can't contain. It's going to burst through the bone and flop onto the balcony like a fish out of water. It'll die out there, the way said water creatures do when they don't have the environment they need.

"All right." Logan comes back out onto the balcony and claps his hands, smiles for miles. "We better get going, or we're going to be late."

I look up from my device, the pristine, pale yellow house on the cover imprinted on the backs of my eyes. In slow-motion, I hold it up and turn it toward him. He looks from my face to the device and falls back a step.

"You write romance novels for a living?" My voice comes out rusty, like I haven't used it in a very long time.

"How did you find out?"

"*You're* L.M. Ryan?"

He puffs out his chest. "I was going to tell you." His voice comes out strong, but there's vulnerability in his eyes, and the two war with each other mightily.

My brain shuts down, but not before sending one last pulse of a sentence to my mouth. "You've been lying to me for years."

Chapter Seventeen
Sloane

I have become my mother. Led to believe one thing when the opposite is true. Not for a week or two, and not something that doesn't really matter like a nickname or how long a person has disliked sushi but has never admitted it until now.

But over the course of years—years! I should've seen this coming. I've kept everything at arm's length until this past week when I opened a door for Logan that no one has been through since the wedding-that-wasn't precisely so this type of thing wouldn't happen to me.

So I wouldn't become like my mother.

In the blink of an eye—Logan Murphy's eye, to be precise—I'm transported back five years.

My wedding dress was pure perfection. The white satin hugged every swell and dip on my body, the fabric falling in full waves from my hips to the ground.

I'd bought bright pink heels, because pink is the color of love, and I've been oh-so-in-love with Leon Burgiss.

I thought he'd loved me too.

His tie matched the shoes—and the lacy bra I wore beneath all the lace and satin. But no one knew that except for me and Leon. Fine, my mom and sisters knew too, but that was all.

When I'd walked down the aisle without my father, with every eye in the world focused on me, I didn't wear the pink heels.

I wore the dress, because I'd literally been tied into it from my butt to my shoulder blades. It would've taken a half an hour to get off, and the wedding was already twenty minutes overdue to begin.

I blink and see Logan standing in front of me. His fingers curl and uncurl into fists, and he's probably asked me something I haven't answered.

He blinks, and I see my dress modeled exquisitely in the window display at the consignment shop where I'd gotten rid of it. I certainly couldn't keep it, though in the history of every wedding, in every country, in every clime, across all ages—that was the one dress meant for and fitted perfectly to a person.

Me.

It sold in a day, and I took the two thousand dollars and opened an online savings account. Because that's what a responsible, put-together woman does. She brushes herself off, puts on a sunny smile and sells houses day after day, and she keeps a pair of pink heels in a box in the back of her closet and wears them on special occasions.

I've worn those heels three times in the past five years, and after the last time, I vowed not to wear them again. They simply hold too many memories I don't want.

Now, Belize will too. This mid-winter trip is forever ruined.

"Sloane," Logan says, unblinking. "You're gone again."

My phone rings, saving me. There are so many things stewing inside, I need time for them to mingle and blend together before I can extract the words I want to say to him.

"It's Rose." I don't want to talk to her, but because I'm one breath away from breaking down, I slide my thumb over the green icon to answer the call.

"Don't answer it," Logan says, but the deed is done. He rolls his eyes—rolls his eyes!—and turns away from me. "Are we going hiking or not?"

"Sloany?" Rose's saying on her end of the line. I feel tied to so many things, so many people. I'm the thumbtack in the middle of a huge cork board, with those colored threads going out to pictures of my mother, my father, each sister, my co-workers, my assistant, my boss, my house, the dog I want, and Logan.

So many strings go to Logan, and most of them are in shades of red. It can represent the color of love, but right now, I feel nothing but heated anger for him.

"Rosy," I say as Logan slides open the glass door to the

room. "I'm on my way out right now. You get two minutes." Surprised by the even, calm tone of my voice, I move to follow Logan. Maybe I won't break down over this.

I blink, and I see my mother standing on my front stoop. Her eyes that day had been bloodshot, her face puffy, her voice the kind that can only be achieved by inhaling copious amounts of helium.

Or finding out your husband of thirty-three years has never loved you.

That he's been cheating on you for at least five years, but probably longer, with a high school girlfriend he's regretted breaking up with for thirty-five years.

Oh, but he's not moving out, and your mother can't stand to sleep in the same house as him, so she needs your guest room "for a day or two."

Which turns into two weeks.

I will not be my mother.

She fell apart and wouldn't talk to my younger sisters until she pulled herself together slightly. The job of keeping everyone informed fell to me, which is why I know all the sordid details I wish I didn't.

I follow Logan inside as Rose says, "This won't take long... Now, I don't want you to freak out, but..." Her voice borders on manic, and if there's anything that can get my sister more animated than a rock, her usual state, it's her boyfriend.

My heart sinks through the floor, down all the levels of this building, and all the way to the beach.

"You got engaged," I say. My tone in no way suggests that I'm excited about this. Rose is twenty-six, which is the same age I was when Leon asked me to marry him. I want to rage at this Spanish-style room. Rip up all the red-orange tiles and scream as I launch them over the balcony, watch them drop three floors, and shatter into pieces below.

I see myself ripping the abstract paintings off the wall and bashing them through the TV that Logan watches soccer on most evenings.

He's waiting for me at the doorway that leads out of the room, and I attempt to brighten as I get closer. "That's so ex—"

"I got engaged!" Rose screams on her end of the line. Thankfully, she doesn't have great lungs. Asthma and all that. So after only two or three seconds, she takes a breath, and she's off to the races.

"I know this will be hard for you, but I need you, Sloany. You planned the absolute perfect wedding for yourself, and I can't even tell the difference between rose and pink. Not that there will be any pink in my wedding."

"Of course not," I say, moving past Logan without truly looking at him. I don't turn back to see if he follows. He had my pack and his on his shoulder, and I can *feel* him behind me. I feel him everywhere, all the time.

It took me a year to stop seeing Leon everywhere I

went. How long until I can't feel Logan with me anymore? And why does that make me so, so sad?

He's been lying to you!

My righteous anger fires up again, and Rose's now saying, "We won't get married until August, so that's lots of time. I know you think I'm too young, but I'm not. I'm done with college. I have a good job, and so does Spencer. It's going to be so great, Sloane. You'll see."

The fact that she has to justify her engagement to me makes my stomach twist. "Of course it will," I say. "Spencer isn't anything like my loser fiancé."

I've always been glad I didn't marry Leon. That didn't make how the relationship ended any easier or any quicker to get over. It also didn't change the fact that I wanted to get married. I wanted that close companionship, the inside jokes, the smiling face when I walk in the door, the implied date on birthdays and Friday nights.

The elevator arrives, and I say, "I'm so sorry. I'm about to get in an elevator. I love you, and we'll talk more tonight, okay?"

"Okay," Rose says, pure sunshine in her voice. "Love you, Sloany!"

Logan holds the door for me so I can lower my phone and get on the car. I smash myself into the corner of the elevator and fold my arms. When the door closes, I'm instantly suffocating, the scent of Logan's skin—like jungle rain and male goodness—and his cologne—all that leather, cider, and musk—closing in on me.

Choking me.

"Sloane," he says. "I write romance novels for a living."

Not just romance novels. The very romance novel I was reading on this trip. The one I just *had* to finish in the hot tub the other night.

Foolishness pulls through me. He's teased me about my reading material in the past. How dare he?

"Why didn't you tell me?" I study the numbers in front of me like they'll rearrange into the MegaLotto winning combination by my sheer will alone.

"It's...not something I've wanted a lot of people to know."

I switch my glare to him. "So I'm just 'some person' now. Okay, got it."

"That's not what I said."

"You didn't tell me!" I've told him everything. I open my mouth, that part of my thoughts solid now. "I've told you everything, Logan. *Everything.* I've bawled in your arms and laid awake with you so many times, spilling my guts."

"I'm aware."

The doors slide open, but I don't move. Those two words, spoken in his deadpan tone, cause ice to flow through my veins where my blood should be.

Logan gets off the elevator, seemingly without knowing I don't go with him. The door starts to slide closed as he turns back. "You're not—?" His voice gets cut off as the door seals.

I lift my phone. *Go without me,* I text

No, he texts back. *Today is our day where we do what the other one wants.*

I grit my teeth. "I don't want to be with you right now." I grunt each word as I type it.

And I want to explain, he says. *You have to give me that much, Sloane. I've been meaning to tell you what I do for months now.*

"Months?" I scoff.

Another message pops up. *Besides, you've never asked what I really do.*

"I've never asked?" He has to be kidding. That's going to be his excuse for mountains of lies? Should my mother have asked my dad if he'd been emailing and calling his high school girlfriend? Do those questions have to be explicitly asked?

The door slides open again, because I haven't pushed a button to go anywhere. Logan stands there, and he sticks his foot out to stall the door from closing again.

"You've never *really* asked," he says, those eyes firing blue sparks at me. Then shots. Then flames.

My chest feels like someone has put a hinge in it in the wrong place. I don't know what to say, and that unnerves me the most. I always know what to say. I'm the one who calms down anxious clients and crying mothers and sisters who've just failed their psychology class.

The elevator starts to sing, and I practically jump off of it. I say nothing as I march past Logan, but his legs are literally twice as long as mine, and he catches up to me easily.

We endure a tense golf cart ride down to the spot where we're meeting the hiking tour group, both of us saying nothing. The silence is thick, like someone has made Jello out of it and encased us in it. I can still see around me, but everything is warped and the color of strawberries.

Only two other people wait in the excursion area, and Logan grabs my hand and pulls me away from them as the golf cart drives off.

"Let me go," I say.

He doesn't, not for a few more steps, and then I manage to wrench my hand away from his. I'm panting, with a pulse that's sprinting from ventricle to ventricle and back. I've never been afraid of Logan Murphy, not even on our first trip. I made a big show out of checking his identification and calling his boss, but he has a trustworthy face.

I keep that to myself right now. "So?" I ask. "Start explaining."

"I've always liked to write." He swallows, and I watch the movement of it in his throat. "I wrote a few novels, and none of them went anywhere. I was in a critique group, and one of the women there said she loved my romance subplot and had I ever considered writing a straight-up romance novel?"

He paces away from me, but when he turns back, his gaze is ironclad. His voice that strong, commanding timbre he uses to get what he wants as he says, "Not sci-fi with a romance thread. All romance. So I gave it a try. I liked it. No, I loved it. I created a new identity, sold a couple of books to a publisher, and then, when they went out of business, I started self-publishing."

"That woman—Alicia—was from Heartfelt Desires."

"Actually, she's my literary agent," he says. "You know like in Jerry Maguire, he's a sports agent for athletes? Authors have agents too."

"I know what a literary agent does," I say dryly. "I'm a real estate *agent*, for crying out loud."

He glares at me, but he honestly has no right. He's mansplaining to me, and he hasn't even gotten to anything good yet.

"My self-published stuff did great. Enough for me to quit that awful job at that textbook company."

"Is that the boss I called five years ago?" My ribs hurt I've been clenching them so tightly.

"Yes. I got a new agent. She sold some more books for me. I still publish quite a few myself. I built a business out of it."

"This is all great," I say, a frown right between my eyes. "I don't understand why you haven't told me."

"For the very reason I witnessed on the balcony," he says. "You were horrified."

"I was not."

"I saw your face. In fact, you still look a little peakish. Your face is gray now instead of white."

"I wasn't horrified because you're an author. I was horrified that you've been *lying* to me for years."

Logan sighs and rolls his head. "Men are not really... your typical romance author. I'm not just an author, Sloane. I write *romance novels.*"

"So what?" I ask.

"You don't get it," he says. "You're a woman. It's fine." He moves past me and adds, "I think our van is here."

"It's not fine." I spin to follow him. "Don't just walk away. Finish the explanation."

He turns back to me so fast I almost ram into his chest. The backpacks swing wildly, and I certainly hope he's remembered to zip them both closed. A can of sunscreen that was tucked into the outer pocket of mine goes clattering to the ground.

We both ignore it, because we're chest-to-chest, eyes blazing, in the parking lot.

Logan's mouth barely moves as he says, "This isn't about *you*, Sloane. It's about me, and how I felt like other people would handle what I do to pay my bills." His eyes are ice cold, as is his tone. In fact, I shiver at the suppressed fury I find behind those chilled blue flames in his gaze.

"It's always been easier to say I owned my own business and leave it at that. People admire that. I don't have to worry about their judgment that way."

Though we stand inches apart, he manages to look down to my feet and back to my face. He definitely doesn't like what he sees, if that lip-curl is anything to judge by.

"Out of everyone, I thought you'd handle it the best. I've been scared but excited to tell you. Your reaction...is *precisely* why I don't tell people. So thanks for confirming that."

He turns and walks away for good now, leaving me to deflate like a blow-up bouncy house that has just had the plug pulled.

Chapter Eighteen
Logan

For two terrifying moments, I think Sloane will stay in the parking lot. She's frozen to the spot, and since I've already gotten in the van, I can't yell at her. The driver takes a few steps toward her, and then thankfully, she thaws and flies into motion.

She exchanges a few words with the driver, then climbs into the van. It's a six-seater, and there are only four of us on this excursion today. She could easily choose to move right past me and sit in the back row all by herself.

I keep my gaze out the window, my heart already in a pile of tiny shredded ribbons. I don't even want to imagine what will happen to my pulse if she doesn't sit beside me. Right now, it booms through my whole body—*boom! Boom! BOOM!*—in the few moments it takes her to decide.

Then the bench seat I'm on shifts, and relief pulls

through me so hard, I hum. I don't know what I mean by it; I barely know I've made a noise at all.

"Please," Sloane mutters as the van door gets slid closed.

I don't really want to continue our argument in front of strangers, so I lean my head back against the rest behind me and close my eyes. I've been up for a couple of hours now, getting newsletters ready to send and dealing with one of my cover designers. Then, of course, Alicia had called, and what should've been amazing news has turned into a giant wedge I can't see past.

I hate celebrating the news that I've sold another novel with myself. My stomach rolls and pitches, because I was literally five minutes away from telling Sloane all about my career.

"You have fifty-two novels?"

I look over to her at her question. She has her blasted phone out, and she lifts that gorgeous face, her pretty baby blues meeting mine. "Wow, Logan."

I look away without answering. Her reaction still cuts through me, the blade the serrated kind that saws at me with every move I make, every thought I have.

I can't believe Alicia called me back. Even worse... "I can't believe you answered my phone," I hiss to her. She had no right to do that.

Without truly looking at her, I cut a look in her direction out of the corner of my eye. Her surprise fades into a look of defiance. Of course. Sloane Sanders is always right.

"She called about a hundred times last night," Sloane says. "I saw her name on your phone then, and I wanted to make sure you weren't cheating on me."

That gets me to turn toward her completely. "Have you lost your mind?"

She only lifts her chin.

"I would *never* do that to you, or anyone else." I laugh bitterly, not even bothering to keep my voice down. "Wow, it's so great to know your real opinion of me, Sloane."

"That's not what I meant."

"Well, then by all means," I say with plenty of sarcasm. "Explain it to me." I glare at her, but she's got a Ph.D. in glaring, so I get it right back.

"I will not be my mother," she says through clenched teeth, a glance to the row in front of us telling me to cool it.

But I don't want to. "That's so great," I say. "Because I'm nothing like your father, Sloane. Or Leon for that matter. Or any of the other men in your life who've let you down. But that doesn't matter. You've already decided that *all* men, inevitably, at some point, won't be good enough for you."

"That is not true."

"Which is why you've let the excuse of being left at the altar guide your life for the past five years. It's why you haven't dated. It's why you didn't see me standing in front of you all this time, begging for some shred of attention from the mighty Queen Sanders."

The man in front of me turns around, but I don't care.

"Stop it," Sloane says. "I'm not the queen."

I'd worship her like one, though. In fact, I have been for over two years now. I clamp my mouth shut, because I've already said some hurtful things, and I don't want to do any more damage.

Still, if she can't see how her reaction and her words have hurt me too, then she really is one of the dumbest smart women I know.

We continue toward the trailhead without a sound in the van. Bit by bit, my anger fades, leaving behind only a chasm of hurt feelings, regret, and guilt too.

Why did Alicia have to call back? Why did Sloane have to answer?

Everything in my body feels too tight. My skin is stitched onto my muscles too tightly. My cells are tense from the nucleus out. Even my hair feels like it's getting pulled right out of my scalp.

The van comes to a stop, and the couple in front of us practically lunge for the door. Sloane slides to the edge of her seat to follow them, but I put my hand on her elbow and murmur, "Sloane," the way I do when I hold her in bed at night.

She turns her head toward me without facing me. "I'm sorry," I say. There are a lot of things to be sorry for, and I'm not exactly sure which one I'm apologizing for. It doesn't matter. I don't want to go on this stupid hike with my best friend mad at me. I can't bear it.

"Can you please shelve your anger with me until we're back to the beach?"

She nods and gets out of the van, turning back to me. She offers me her hand and I take it when I reach the end of the bench seat. I don't need her help getting out, but I know what this is.

A temporary peace offering.

"I'm sorry too," she says. "I don't think you're like my father."

"You kind of do, though." I get out and stand next to her. "Never mind. I shouldn't have said that." Even if it is true.

Not everything that's true needs to be said. In fact, most of the loudest voices out there aren't speaking the truth at all. They're just talking to hear themselves talk. They're loud, and relentless, and hardly ever right.

"Let's just get through the next one-point-three miles," she says, hitching her backpack up on her shoulders like she's facing an army of demons singlehandedly.

I know she doesn't like hiking, but I did choose the easiest, shortest hike—and one that ends with the best view. So I say nothing as we follow the guide. He speaks to us about the foliage and the wildlife here, how the jungles are used and preserved here in Belize, and dozens of other random facts I'd probably be interested in any other time.

Right now, thoughts of the things I should've told Sloane on our balcony flood through my mind. In my books, the hero always knows the right thing to say, and he possesses the bravery to say it. Of course, the heroine gives him the page time to say it, and I can cut her off any time I want in order for him to *be* the hero.

I feel very unheroic as we return to the resort and then enter our room. "All right," I say with a sigh. I didn't exactly break a sweat out there, and I flop onto the bed. "Are we going to the beach right away?"

Sloane doesn't answer, and the bathroom door clicks closed in the next moment. I exhale, and my first thought is to simply slip out while she's in there. We have phones, and of course, I have to sleep here for the next two evenings.

Instead, I stay right where I am. I'm tired of running from hard conversations, the idea of hurting her feelings—or mine—and her.

I'm not going to run from her anymore.

When she comes out of the bathroom, I sit up and meet her eye. "Sloane."

She seems surprised that I'm still there, and that doesn't comfort me. My past track record shrieks through me—I've always run from her. I've let her dictate everything between us, and me staying here when she clearly wanted me to leave isn't in our paradigm of normal.

"What's the first thing you'd ask someone if they told you they were an author?" I ask.

She gives me a wary glance as she passes. She goes all the way to the end of the dresser and then perches on it.

The air around her radiates tension, and it pulls around her eyes too.

"Listen," I say. "We're not sixteen years old. We're adults, and we can have this conversation."

Her lips purse slightly, and then she presses them together, almost like she has something to say and is holding it back. I give her a moment, but she remains silent. I sigh, because this isn't the woman I know. "You don't have anything to say?"

Irritation fires across her face, making her nostrils flare slightly. She won't look away from me now, and I find myself as equally drawn to her. Her mouth opens, and she says, "I thought you told me everything, Logan. It hurts to know that that was only one-sided."

"It wasn't," I say. "You're the only person I've shared my life with in the past five years."

She shakes her head. "Then I should've known this."

"Yeah," I say. "You should've, and some of that is on you. I had plans to tell you, and when Alicia called to tell me I've just sold two more books, I thought that was the perfect opening. I'd tell you about *Heartfelt* buying the books, and we'd celebrate today in a big way."

That's all ruined now, and I wish I was in my sad house in Superior, alone. I'd get Titan a frozen marrow bone, and I'd order the deep dish pizza I like. Among ham, pepperoni, mushrooms, and green peppers, I'd toast myself for a job well done.

It's a pathetic picture, and unfortunately, one I've lived already.

"You write beachy romances," she says. "Are our trips research for you?"

No point in lying about it. "Yeah, sure," I say. "Every day is research for me. You think I can come up with the things in my books from pure imagination?" I shake my head. "Fiction is born from real life. It has to feel authentic to resonate with people. With readers."

She tilts her head and considers me, a measure of confusion riding in her gaze. She's looked at me like this before. The first time was when I stepped next to her at the ticketing agent's desk and said I needed a ticket to Mexico. One of her honeymoon tickets.

"What did you like about *Love at Sunset*?" I ask.

She blinks a couple of times. "Belinda was so…"

"Real," I say. "She had problems, and for a few chapters there, you aren't sure if you like her. Right?"

Sloane doesn't confirm, but she doesn't need to. I know Belinda's story—it's every woman's story. "Readers do wonder about her," I say. "But in the end, they adore her, and they start to cheer for her. Not only that, but the only person in the world who can make her happy—who completes her in a way she didn't know she needed to be completed—is Rocko."

Her hero.

She nods. "I got teary when they got back together at the end."

"That makes me so happy," I murmur. "That's the exact reaction I want readers to have."

"Have you taken things from me and put them in your books?" She wears an expression halfway between hope and horror, and I'm not sure how to answer. Complete honesty might have me back in the lobby, begging for a different room.

But I can't lie to her.

"Yes," I say, my throat already raw. "Since I met you, Sloane, every single book I've written has had part of you in it."

Her eyes widen, but she says nothing.

I can stop there, but for some reason, I don't. "There's the story you told me about how you met Leon in a book called Waterfall's Edge. I know you don't want to be reminded of it, but it was pretty romantic." I give her a small smile she doesn't return.

My chest feels like a cave, with sharp objects growing from the top and bottom of it. Somehow, the air makes it past all the jagged pieces and into my lungs. Then out. "I wrote a whole book about a real estate agent once. I had one of my couples take a trip to South Carolina after we went."

"You loved the beaches there," she murmurs.

"My career was nothing when I met you," I say. "I had just started in romance, and I wasn't sure if I was any good at it. Then I met you, and I...came alive. I put the funny things you text me in one book, and all your favorite foods in another. I wrote a book about a woman who wanted a dog so badly but could never get one because of you."

I should stop talking, but I can't seem to make the tide of words stop. "I know you want perfection, but Sloane, no one's perfect. I'm never going to be that man. I can't guarantee that our lives won't be messy. I think life is *supposed* to be messy. It's supposed to be a maze, and all we can hope for is that we find someone who's willing to lock arms with us and never let go."

She looks away, but the thick, red curtains are still closed from this morning.

"I'd try to make your dreams come true," I whisper. "I really would, but it's exhausting knowing that I'm going to fail. That I'll never be good enough for you."

"Logan, you're good enough for me." She doesn't sound terribly convincing, though when Sloane speaks in that quiet voice, her head down, I generally believe her.

I lay back on the bed and close my eyes. "I'm so tired. This trip was supposed to be relaxing, and it's been the opposite of that."

"Has it?"

"Yes."

"Why? Because of this?"

"Because," I say. "I've been carrying heavy things for a long time, all by myself. I finally told you how I feel about you, and that was a huge weight off my shoulders. But then, I had to balance that with sleeping in the same bed as you and not taking things too far. Because I don't want to lose you before I've even had you, and I know you're not ready. And yes, this. I've been trying to find a way to tell you, and it just hadn't come forward yet."

She remains quiet, which pushes a pin of annoyance into my heart. She can at least acknowledge that my feelings are valid, and that this trip has been unique in the fact that we've been crammed together in the same room for almost ten days. The same bed. And we've been kissing.

In all, this trip is wholly unlike our others.

"I've been looking at apartments and long-term vacation rentals in Pittsburgh for six months," I say. "I have a tab open on my laptop right now, because I was looking at them this morning when Alicia called."

I keep my eyes closed, because it's so much easier to talk this way. Sloane was right on the first night here. It's easier to share things with the lights off, when there's no one watching, and no facial cues to read, and no body language to interpret.

"I can't guarantee you perfection," I say. "But I would never cheat on you, and I'd vacuum your SUV, and I believe we'd find a way to make things work when they got messy, because we love each other."

"Murph."

"But I can't be expected to be perfect." I sit up and look at her. She seems one breath away from either going postal or breaking down. At this point, I'm not sure which I prefer. There's not much left in my gas tank to comfort her, but I also can't dodge any of her attacks either.

"I think it's really unfair of you to expect me to be perfect."

She frowns. "I never said I did."

"You did, though."

She gathers her honeyed hair into a ponytail and secures it with a band. She doesn't go back on her dream of perfection, and she doesn't apologize for it either. I don't really expect her to, because this is Sloane, and I know exactly who she is.

She's unwavering in what she wants, and she will work herself to the bone to achieve it. In this case, however, she can't have the impossible dream without another human being, and she can't control them. She can't simply work more hours or get another certification, and then *presto!* she's got an unwavering, perfect husband.

Life doesn't work that way, not even in romance novels.

I'm so tired, and my stomach is growling. I have to get out of this room, and I fully expect Sloane to simply let me leave. After getting to my feet and checking for my keycard, I say, "I'm gonna go."

"Go where?"

"I don't know. I just need to think for a bit."

She doesn't protest, and I step over to the door. I turn back to her, finding her exquisitely beautiful, the way I always have. She seems childlike right now, almost smaller than she normally is, her spirit held very close to her as she works through something difficult for her.

"Sometimes Sloane, love has to be enough to bridge the gaps between what you want and what someone else can give. Love is what makes impossible things possible."

Then I open the door and leave. I haven't exactly told her I love her, but I also definitely told her I love her.

"More than once," I mutter as I stride away from the suite. To my dismay, Sloane doesn't come after me.

Chapter Nineteen
Sloane

I keep my eyes closed as I listen to the fussy babies on the airplane. They've actually been comforting me on this flight, because I've been able to daydream about what traveling might be like with a child of my own.

The space between the window and my seat is too wide for me to comfortably rest my head, but it's strange to cuddle into Logan now. Which makes no sense. On the trip here, we were "just friends," and I sank into his warmth and embrace like it was a hot sauna and my bones the weariest on the planet. This is only the first leg of our trip, and we'll have to go through the international terminal, pick up our luggage, and go through the domestic security gate in Atlanta.

From there, we'll part, and my heart squeezes like it's been put in one of those garlic minces. Whoever is on the outside of it is mashing, smashing, and trying with all their might to get my arteries and veins to come out as rice on the other side.

It hurts. I hurt all over, and not just from the 1.3-mile hike. But from the past two days of trying not to talk to Logan when all I want to do is talk to Logan.

If I remember correctly, and I do have to rely on my memory, because Logan and I haven't discussed our itineraries lately, his flight is a couple of hours before mine.

He's going to Minneapolis, where he'll have to drive a couple of hours home to Superior. I'm flying into Pittsburgh, and we should be walking through our respective front doors about the same time.

In years past, we'd text each other that we made it home safely. I'd tell him I wish I had a dog, and he'd send me selfies of him and Titan. Tonight, I'm not expecting any texts from Logan.

The plane jams into the ground, and I gasp and then yelp, my eyes flying open. Logan actually throws out an arm to keep me from bashing my head against the seat back in front of me, and I curse myself for feigning sleep during landing.

Logan looks at me, his gaze somewhere else and lowers his arm when he apparently realizes I'm not going to smash my head open. I pluck my phone from the pocket and turn off the airplane mode, but no texts flood in.

It's Sunday, and even busy real estate agents take some days off. Logan's phone chimes, and that only serves to remind me that I'm going to meet a dark, chilly end to today all by myself.

I always hate the end of this trip, and this one is especially excruciating. Pure misery threads through me, leaving an end that someone will be able to tug on and then pull. Every minute that passes adds another stitch, all of them getting tighter and more braided together.

Beside me, Logan chuckles, his thumbs flying across his screen. I don't want to look at his phone, but I can't help it. I catch the name of his sister, and before I can censor myself, I smile.

Hattie is funny, if he's to be believed, and he's putting that evidence on display. He straightens his mouth and cuts me that sexy look out of the corner of his eye. I quickly look away too, pretending I'm entranced by the view beyond the window.

I lift the shade and get blinded, somehow forgetting that we've landed in the South, and it's nowhere near dark yet. I groan and squish my eyes closed.

"Do you still want to get lunch here?" Logan asks, releasing his seatbelt before the indicator goes off. He's always been a bit of a rule-breaker in that regard, and I glance toward the front of the plane, expecting the ultra-stern flight attendant to start wagging her finger. No one appears, and the plane continues to taxi toward whatever gate we've been assigned.

"Yes," I say a bit breathlessly. "Do you know what gate you're at yet?"

"E-terminal," he says. "But it doesn't matter. We can go through security together and ride the train wherever we need to go."

"The train is always too hot," I complain.

"True," he says. We almost always fly through Atlanta, because we've always gone somewhere tropical—or at least warmer than the four degrees I'm returning to in Pittsburgh—for our trip.

The ding sounds, and the clanking, metallic sound of seatbelts getting released fills the cabin. People jump to their feet and crowd into the aisle, as if they can get off the plane right this second. I'm in the window seat, so I stay right where I am.

Logan unfolds his tall frame as he stands, but he has to scrunch his shoulders and bend his head under the overhead compartment. For a flash, a brief moment of time, our eyes meet and it's like the past ten days haven't happened yet.

He's getting off his connecting flight to Atlanta, and he'll be waiting for me at the baggage claim. Since I've had to stop to use the restroom and buy a treat, he's got my bag, and my emotions fizz through my blood as I try to figure out why I'm thinking about his shoulders and how big his hands are.

By the time we get off the plane, I can't stand the way we've been shuffling around. Shifting our feet in smaller steps than I'd like, just to give the person in front of us more room. Doing a delicate dance, so I don't touch Logan in any way that he might misconstrue.

I want to spread my arms as wide as they'll go and start running. Of course, I don't run; I think I've proven that on more than one occasion.

The Atlanta airport is a bustling place, with tens of thousands of people just trying to get somewhere else. After all, no one's final destination is ever an airport, and most of us want to move through the lines in the bathroom, at the Starbucks or McDonalds, and security as seamlessly as possible.

Because then we get where we really want to go. Vacation. Home. To see a loved one we've known our whole lives, or perhaps to meet someone we've fallen for on a dating app and have never met in the flesh.

No matter what, I let my arms do their natural back and forth as I walk beside Logan. His strides are naturally longer than mine, but he goes at my pace. I wonder if he ever feels held back, and if it drives him as crazy as it's driving me right now.

We sit down at Rooster's, an American-style diner that serves fried chicken, burgers, and the best French fries I've ever eaten in my life. I want to order a plate of them and nothing else and eat the whole thing by myself. At the same time, I can't stand to separate from Logan quite yet.

"Okay, look," I say, ignoring the menu on the table in front of me. Happier couples than Logan and I sit at the tables around us, and waiters and waitresses flit around. A steady stream of people walks by, passes through, all of them with some other destination than here.

I want to be right here, right now. This has to be resolved before he heads to whatever E-gate he's at and I figure out how badly I've messed up with him.

"The last couple of days have been tense."

Logan simply looks at me, not arguing but not saying it hasn't been that bad. It has been, and we both know it. Him probably more than me, as he spent the last two nights of his vacation on a lounge chair that doesn't lay all the way flat. He was too tall for it, and his feet hung off the end or he had to bend his body into an S-shape to fit.

"But we always have a destination for our next mid-winter trip before we go home. Can we—?" My voice quits on me, and I don't even know why. I clear my throat and find I still have vocal cords. A quick glance around shows that no one cares what I was about to say.

Logan watches me, and I tell myself that he cares. He does. He's just going off my cues, and I'm a basket case right now. I hate that I am, and I just need to get back to my routine, and my thoughts and emotions will fall into line too.

Then I'll know why, even after he explained why, it still feels like Logan has been lying to me for far too long.

"Can we just choose a destination?" I swipe on my phone, so I have something to look at. "We can change it later. I don't care. I just want something to be like it usually is."

Logan exhales slowly, obviously trying not to sigh. But he's totally sighing, and it's one that says, *Fine, Sloane. You and your silly routines.*

I tap to open my map, and I pinch out until I can practically see the whole world. "What are you thinking? Domestic or foreign?"

He considers for a moment. "We wanted to do domestic this year. Perhaps that."

I nod, because we can both afford the trip. Him more than I even knew. Fifty-two books, and while I have no idea how to tell if they're selling well, he did just land another book deal.

We had gone to the beach, but there had been no storytelling in his sultry voice. Once I knew he told stories —he literally makes up lies—for a living, I couldn't ask him to give me one for free.

I'd kept my cover-up on, because I didn't want to ask Logan to lotion my shoulders and back. I'd ended up falling asleep, and Logan had to wake me so we could go get dinner.

"Texas?" I ask. "Galveston is an island."

"Is it warm in January?"

"I don't know." I drag the map somewhere else. "We could just try Florida again."

"Sure," he says, and I know he won't choose.

"Or Jamaica," I say. "The Dominican Republic. Or Guatemala."

"Not Central America," he says. "That's the rule."

He's right. Last year, after we went to Grand Cayman one year, then St. Lucia the very next, we made a rule that we should mix up our geographic regions. We'd originally started out by saying we couldn't do back-to-back trips on the same continent, but we have done domestic trips back-to-back, and that's technically the same continent.

So we made it more broad by saying *region*. Both Grand Cayman and St. Lucia are in the Caribbean, so this year we chose Florida. Close, but not really the Caribbean. Belize we labeled Central America, which does mean Guatemala is out.

"It doesn't have to be the beach," he says. "Right?"

"Right," I say evasively, though I much prefer the beach. Who wants to feel like they've been put into an oven to bake?

"What about New Mexico?" he asks.

"Sure," I say, mimicking him from a few minutes ago. If he notices, he doesn't say anything.

A waiter appears to take our order, and I ask for a bacon cheeseburger and the seasoned fries I love so much. Oh, and a strawberry lemonade. I never drink anything but water and diet cola at home, and I want one last fruity drink before I go on my next year-long fast from them.

Once he's gone, Logan meets my eyes. His dance with amusement, and I'm once again hopeful that we aren't completely broken. "You would die in New Mexico."

"Then why did you suggest it?"

"To see what you would say."

I roll my neck, wondering when I started to feel like I'd been yoked to him.

"Let's plan on Florida," he says, and I nod, because I don't care where we go. I just want a destination on the calendar.

The conversation stalls there, and it isn't until our food arrives that he says, "I have to get going soon, but I have a question for you, if you don't mind."

"Depends on what it is." He gives me that cold-fire look, and I wave a fry in his direction. "Fine. Go ahead."

"If I hadn't...told you how I felt about you, would you have acted on your feelings?"

I note the use of "felt," and it makes my most vital organ squeeze too tightly and try to shoot up my throat. Does he not still feel romantic things for me?

"What do you mean?" I ask, because I need a minute to riddle through all he's said and what he means by it. I wish I could peel back just a flap of his gorgeous hair and see inside his head. Even when he explains things, I'm not sure I understand, and that's all on me. It would be so much easier if I could simply see his thoughts, his motivations, his assumptions, all laid out on paper. Then, when I get confused or I start to second-guess or my irrational hour comes, I can be reminded in black and white of what's true and what's not.

"I mean, Sloane." He finishes chewing his own hamburger and swipes his napkin across his mouth. "You said you had feelings for me when you saw me at baggage claim. If I hadn't said anything to you last week, would you have done anything about them? On this trip?"

"I don't know."

He nods, his face closing off with every moment that passes. I see the windows fly closed, the door slam shut and get locked, and all the storm shutters draw down, latching into place to keep the hurricane out. To keep things from getting broken by wind, rain, and acts of God.

We eat in that horrible silence that's plagued us a few times on this trip. Once we finish and pay, Logan stands and shoulders his pack. "I have to get going. My plane is about to board, and I still have to get over to the gate."

I lunge to my feet and throw myself into his arms. "I'm so sorry, Logan. For everything."

He grips me tightly, holds me close against his strong, broad chest. "Sloane, I just need you to figure out what you want me to do." He inches back a little. Enough for him to touch his forehead to mine. "Okay? You know I'm going to do whatever you want me to do."

Logan steps back completely, his eyes electric now. "But Sloane, I need to know the answer to what I asked, and 'I don't know' doesn't work for me."

"But I don't know."

He nods, his mouth drawing itself into a grim line. "I'm just going to say this, and you can do with it what you want." He clears his throat, no hum resonating in my eardrums. "I'm not sure you would've acted on anything you felt if I hadn't first confessed my crush."

My heartbeat starts to hammer, but I don't have a comeback for what he's said. He's not done talking, either, so I stay silent.

Through the pounding of my pulse in my ears, I hear him say, "And I don't want to be the man you like simply because he liked you first." A flashing smile comes to his face and disappears in a cloud of hurt, which he also wipes away before I can really grasp what I'm seeing.

"Logan."

He presses his lips to mine right there in Rooster's, and the kiss is soft and slow for only two strokes before he pulls away. "Just…" He shakes his head, nods to me, and walks away.

I watch him, because I have no other choice. He has to make his flight, and I have to make a lot of decisions.

Falling back into my chair at the table, not even the best French fries on the planet can comfort me now. I still pick one up absently and swipe it through the spiced ketchup. As I eat it, I think about what Logan's asked me. All he's said.

I don't want to be the guy you like simply because he liked you first.

That's not true. That's not who he is.

Is it?

Chapter Twenty
Sloane

T he hours blur into streaks of navy and gray. Sometimes white, as we descend into Pittsburgh as only one of the bright white things falling from the sky. The snowstorm whips the plane to the left so violently, several passengers cry out in fear.

I make no noise at all. I feel like I've left my voice in Atlanta, attached to Logan's backpack as one of the pins he collects from all the places he travels. He buys one in every city he visits, including all of the trips we've taken together.

The snowstorm forces us to do a sliding landing that I'm sure will end with us creating a fiery ball of plane parts, backpacks, snorkeling flippers, and cellphone SIM cards.

Somehow, the pilots get us to stop before we ram into the airport, and a quiet desperation rises up inside me to get off this airplane. I drove myself to the airport, because my flights are never on time, and I didn't want to have to text my mom or my sister about when I'd be arriving. The back and forth at the end of a trip is too much for me, and I've learned that I prefer to drive myself and park in the long-term lot.

That means I'll have to wait for a shuttle after getting my own bag from the carousel, and dread that weighs as much as several tons of bricks settles in my stomach.

"Local time is eight-forty-seven p.m.," the pilot parrots at us as if everyone on this plane hasn't already re-activated their data connections. "Temperature is a balmy one degree, with winds at eleven miles per hour out of the southeast. It's currently snowing, and if Pittsburgh is your final destination, you've likely got your coats and gloves out already."

At this very funny joke, he gives a chuckle. I look up the aisle as if he'll be standing there, on display like a stand-up comedian. Even the flight attendants can't be seen.

"We're currently waiting for another plane to push back from our gate, and then we'll get you on your way."

"Can they even take off in this weather?" the man next to me grumbles.

"I doubt it," says the man on the end. My bladder screams at them to get out of the way so I can make a beeline for the restroom. I haven't stepped over them one time on this flight, and my patience clearly has more to it than I thought, because I remain still and silent.

Two more assurances from the pilot that we'll be getting to our gate "any minute now" have us still sitting on the tarmac. The babies start fussing, and internally, I add my voice to theirs.

Finally, the plane moves, and we roll up to a gate. The dinging happens, and it's like an explosion of released breath happens with every single passenger on the jet. People leap to their feet, and clicks, clatters, and clearing of throats fill the air in a cacophony of sound.

Again, I am still and silent, like a boulder in a raging river. All the water, the fish, the life flows around me in a rush of sound and whiteness. I've existed like this before, and I imagine my eyes to be the big cartoon-character kind, wide and pathetic, with shiny tears filling the bottom third.

No one looks at me. When it's my turn to get out and enter the aisle, a couple from the row behind me goes first. I just let them. I don't care.

I walk, my legs knowing how to do what they were made to do. My lungs continue to inhale-exhale, but I don't count the breaths to find my core or calm down. I'm the calmest I've ever been.

I'm like the walking dead—and no one wants to get too close to a zombie.

I just need to get my second ticket refunded.

Maybe someone else can use it if they won't refund it.

I'm going to Mexico alone.

I start when I realize that my thoughts have flown back in time five years. The human mind is funny that way, and while most of the time I love accessing my memories, these are a few I don't particularly ever want to experience again.

The last time I felt this detached from my body was when I'd taken my pre-packed bag and driven myself to the airport for my non-honeymoon trip. The day I met Logan Murphy.

I stop right in the middle of the wide walkway which the gates line. People flow around me, the blonde boulder standing in their way. The black faux-leather seats around me are filled with people. At every gate. Everywhere I look.

As I stand there, color bleeds back into my retinas. Murph has been painting in vibrant strokes every day since I met him, and I wonder when I first started to fall in love with him. In Mexico that first year?

With the hundreds and then thousands of texts and phone calls since?

Last year, I remember looking at him fondly over a pot of melted cheese as he made a face filled with doubt and wariness, then dunked the sliced pear into it and put it in his mouth. He'd eaten it, but he hadn't liked it. I'd laughed and laughed, and then I'd eaten all the pears.

Did I love him then?

"I think I did," I whisper to the movement around me.

I don't like him just because he liked me first. "And so what if I do?" I ask. My chest pinches, and I take a deep breath, thinking maybe my lungs have forgotten to do their job while I've been deep inside my gray matter.

"Isn't that how relationships work?" They're not even, I know that. I loved Leon with my whole heart, and he wasn't even in the same arena as me. On the spectrum of love, he was on step one, and I was on one hundred.

Love is a sliding scale, and sometimes a person moves quickly, and sometimes they don't. Logan has entertained feelings for me for two years, his clicker moving up the love scale slowly but surely, until he couldn't keep things quiet anymore.

Just because I didn't arrive there first doesn't mean I love him any less. Maybe my clicker moved quickly once he'd confessed his feelings, because I didn't have to cage them behind careful texts and suppression ropes made of doubt. He did, but that doesn't mean I have to.

It also doesn't mean I did anything wrong.

I take my next step just as someone comes over the loudspeaker. "Ladies and gentlemen, we here at the Pittsburgh Airport regret to inform you that air traffic control has just closed the airport."

A loud, collective groan rises up, followed by grumbles and a few people yelling out. I realize how lucky I am to be on the ground; my flight might have been one of the very last ones to touch down.

I immediately want to tell Logan and find out where

he is and if his flight went okay. He should be driving, but he's never had an issue responding. He told me once that his SUV has all the fancy bells and whistles, and he can do voice commands.

Mine's the same, and something warm flickers inside my chest. I don't know what it is, and I don't know what it means, but I want to talk to Logan. Tell him about my horrible flight, all the things I've been thinking about, and ask him to please help me reason through my feelings.

First, I need to get away from this airport before they stop running the shuttles to the long-term parking lot.

When I walk through my front door, I'm not sure there's been a time I've been happier to be home. I had to wait through four shuttles until there was room for me, and I slid into two curbs on my drive home.

But I'm here now.

I drag my suitcase over the final lip of the doorway and tap to close it with my foot. It swings closed and slams shut. I automatically reach behind me to twist the locks, and I take a deep, deep breath.

It even smells like home here, like I did a fresh load of laundry right before I left and then burned a candle labeled *Powdered Sea Salt*. I think of Logan—what else is new?—and what his cologne would do if mingled with the smells here.

I think the musky notes of his skin, and the fresh crispness of his hair would fit right in. The leather and cider from his cologne would marry well with the powder, calming it even, the way he does me when I get into a frenzied state.

Like I am now.

I have to talk to him, and I have no reason to delay it any longer. I pluck my phone from my purse and tap to dial his number. Just then, I hesitate. Maybe I should start with a text instead.

Made it home, and let me tell you, that was by the skin of my teeth. I think my flight was the last one into Pittsburgh. They closed the airport before I even got to baggage claim.

I don't need to cram everything into one message, so I send that one, my thumbs already flying across the screen to compose another. I've texted him like this before, and usually, he calls me already laughing.

How was your flight? The drive to Superior? Are you home yet?

Three questions in a row feels like a lot, and I force my fingers to stop there. Logan needs to respond before I say anything else, and I tuck my phone away and take my suitcase down the hall and into my master suite.

I have to be at work tomorrow, and I should dump the entire contents of my suitcase into the washing machine so I can move it to the dryer before I have to go to bed. I love unpacking right after I get home, because then I don't have a chore hanging over my head when I need to be searching the MLS for a client's dream home.

Tonight, I don't have the energy to do much more than stare at my phone, willing Logan to respond. When he doesn't after several long seconds, I plug in my phone, leave my suitcase in front of my closet, and start shedding my clothes. I step into the shower, sure I'll have all the answers to my questions and the whole spiel of his journey back to Superior when I get out.

"We're here!" Rose calls from the front of the house, and I wipe my hands on the apron tied around my waist. My eyes skate across the screen of my phone, which sits dark and blank. Logan hasn't texted since Monday, and even then, it was to say, *Made it home safely. Glad you did too.*

Eight words.

He hasn't texted since, and I'm trying not to count the days. It's been four.

Or the hours. One hundred and ten, if someone asks, though. Each one has felt astronomically long, and just when I don't think I'll be able to endure another one, I do. The human heart is the most amazing thing in the whole universe, because it can love as deep as the darkest trench in the ocean, and yet hurt so much, a woman feels like she's buried inside that chasm.

She can't breathe. She can't think. She can't imagine

that anyone, including the man she's pretty sure she loves, will be able to find her. She doesn't even know where she is herself.

And yet, the heart beats on.

Just when I think today might finally be the day my heart can't take any more, my younger sister appears at the end of the hall. She's carrying a binder at least four inches thick, with fabrics in various textures and patterns spilling from the seam.

"Are these the linens?" I reach for and take the binder from her. It weighs a couple of pounds at least, and I lay it open on my dining room table. A pretty burgundy looks back at me, but I would never let Rose do dark colors for her wedding luncheon.

She doesn't want that anyway. She has the emotional range of a cup of coffee, which is to say that she pleases people a great deal, but when she's bitter, people spit her right back out. Thankfully, she's found someone who knows how to sweeten her up, pour in the right amount of cream, or a shot of flavoring, and moan as he tastes her again.

"I'm thinking blue," Rose says, crowding in close beside me.

"Mm."

"A light blue," she clarifies, turning. She enters the kitchen and lifts the lid on the pot on the stove. "Is this cabbage patch stew?"

"It's ten degrees outside," I say in my defense.

"It's cabbage and tomatoes." The lid clatters as she replaces it. Her footsteps march over to me. "Okay, tell me what's going on."

I force myself to lazily flip a page in the binder, and then another. None of these are blue, and I wait until I'm sure my features are perfectly schooled into the exact expression I want Rose to see before I look at her.

"It's terribly cold," I say. "And I happen to like that soup."

"It's Dad's recipe."

"It's Grandma's." I turn another page and finally reach the navies. "And what are we supposed to do? Cut out everything that Dad even breathed on once? He's still our father. I can make his recipe." Besides, I half the chili powder, because I don't want all that spice. Just a hint of heat is good enough for me.

"Mom's on her way here."

I jerk my eyes to Rose's. "What? Why?"

"She said she wanted to have lunch with us, and since I couldn't get you out of your house, she said she'd come here."

"My SUV has that check engine light on," I say. It's not a lie, but it's also not a reason why I'd normally cancel lunch with my sister. It's all the people out there I don't want to see. It's the fact that I don't want to paint on my face for a sixth day in a row, smile at waitresses who want me to order a lot so they'll get a bigger tip, and gush over the intricate shades of blue before a dessert menu is asked for and then the sweet treats are bypassed so Rose will fit into her wedding dress in eight months' time.

Me? I'd take all the dessert in the world now, but I've made cabbage, tomato, and ground beef stew. It's diet food, but Rose doesn't comment on that.

"Well, she's going to be here in about twenty minutes," Rose says. "So you better tell me what's really going on before that happens."

Another flip of another page. Another second ticks by on the clock. It'll turn into a minute, then another hour.

It'll be number one hundred and eleven since I've heard from Logan.

I can't school my emotions again, so I look at Rose with high eyebrows and a shaky bottom lip. "I'm just furious I'm here instead of somewhere warm."

Rose nods like what I've said is the reason I've been pacing the floors at night, counting seconds, minutes, and hours. The cold can drive a person to madness, that's for sure. People try to ward against it with wool socks and mittens with sewn-in pockets for heat warming packets of chemicals.

They put on hats with earflaps and tug them down tightly, but the cold is just like madness, which is just like the capability of the human heart. It never ends; it simply seeps through the tiniest of cracks, reminding you that your best friend and the man you most likely love hasn't texted you back for going on five days now.

The timer on my stove goes off, indicating that the

stew has boiled long enough to marry all the flavors together. It's been another hour.

I brush past my sister to turn off the beeping. She says, "It's Logan."

My feet freeze before I can tell them to keep going. Smooth. *I'm Smooth Sloane, and nothing ruffles me,* I coach myself.

Rose darts in front of me before I can get myself moving again. "It's Logan Murphy." She looks into my eyes, and I have no idea what she sees, but her blue-green eyes—she got some of Dad's genes more prevalently than I do—fill with compassion, like someone has put real cane sugar in her coffee.

"You're in love with him." She cradles my face in one hand. "Oh, honey, when did you fall in love with him? And what happened in Belize?"

Chapter Twenty-One
Logan

The snow moves with the force of the shovel, unable to resist the pressure I apply to the handle. I'm sweating beneath my coat and hat, and underneath my scarf. Even inside my gloves. Mother Nature seems to want to bury the entire state of Wisconsin under mountains of snow, leaving those of us trying to eek out an existence to try to clear the walkways and driveways and roads.

I've done my own driveway and front sidewalk, and I'm a few shovelfuls away from having my parents' clean and clear too. They aren't going anywhere, but then the grocery delivery will be able to pull in and take the plastic bags up to the front door without slipping or getting soaked in the process.

The sky isn't storming today, but it's not blue either. It exists in shades of gray and white, the clouds shapeless and unformed. It reminds me of myself since returning from Belize. It's been two weeks, and Valentine's Day is in only two days.

Before Belize, I'd entertained fantasies of flying to Pittsburgh and dropping by Sloane's place—somewhere I have never been and don't even know the address for—for a spontaneous dinner. Of course, I haven't made any plans, because I was waiting to see how things went in Belize. If I'd be brave enough to tell her how I feel, and to see how she'd react to the news. If she'd box me back into the friend zone or if she'd hold my hand, kiss me, and giggle quietly with me while we cuddle on a single lounger with the Central American sun giving us its blessing.

I sigh and focus. Fantasies are exactly that—unreal. A figment of imagination, dreamed up by a hopeless man who probably should've kept his mouth shut.

I finish the driveway and call, "Come on, Titan." I follow that with a whistle and the dog barks from somewhere down the block. "Come on!"

My canine comes racing around the corner, his joy unaffected by the snow. I wish I was more like him, and I can't help chuckling and scrubbing him down as he skids to a stop in front of me. Titan goes between my legs so I can scratch the one-inch area where his tail meets his body, which I happily do.

"Come on," I say. "I'm done here. Let's go in." Together, we head inside. The interior of my mother's house smells equally like cocoa and coffee, and I'm sure while I've been shoveling, she's been mixing. After shedding my winter gear near the door so I don't drip on her carpet, I glance at my father, snoozing in his recliner. In the kitchen, I find a thick pan stuffed to the top with Rice Crispy treats, and I wonder when my mom thought I'd started aging backward.

"How'd it go?" she asks as she bustles into the kitchen.

"It's winter," I say like that answers the question. I lift my backpack to the dining room table. "Can I stay for dinner? I just have a few things to do on the computer." I glance over to her, but I can't quite look at her fully. "And, uh, I have some news for you and Dad."

"You can stay as long as you want," Mom says, as I knew she would. If it were up to her, I'd move back in here, never to leave again. Never to be married. Never to have a son of my own.

I don't mean to, but I sigh as I pull my laptop out and open it. Sitting heavily in my seat, I use my fingerprint to unlock the machine, and I find myself staring at the last thing I'd been doing on my machine.

Looking at rentals in Pittsburgh.

My heart tears right in half, but the problem is, it's already done that every day since I walked away from Sloane in the Atlanta airport. The miles I've walked and run since then have felt endless, and no matter how hard I pound my feet into the treadmill, I can't outrun VRBO. I can't just stop thinking about Sloane and planning a life that puts the two of us in the same city.

Because maybe then...

I know what comes after this part of the thought, and I can't stop myself from the way the words roll through my head. I'm literally in the business of words, and normally, I'm stoked I have so many.

Maybe then, we can keep dating.

Maybe then, she'll have the time she needs to fall in love with me the way I've fallen for her.

Maybe then, I won't see her for ten days out of three hundred sixty-five, and we'll have a real chance of building a future together.

I can't do it from here, and yet, I haven't taken a single step to do anything different than what I've been doing for the past two years. I haven't even been able to allow myself to text Sloane back. She's likewise gone silent, and I hate that. A Silent Sloane is a Thinking Sloane, and her thoughts can get really deep and really irrational really fast.

I have first-hand experience with that now, as much as I wish I didn't.

"You're moving to Pittsburgh?" A plate of crispy treats falls to the table beside me, dislodging the sweets and making them jump and bobble.

I slam my laptop closed and meet my mother's eye. She has one palm pressed to her heart, her mouth hanging open as she draws in short breaths and puffs them out.

"Mom." I jump to my feet. "I don't want to explain it twice."

"Larry!" she yells, her eyes still locked on mine.

"He's napping," I say. "I was planning to talk to you both over dinner." Can nothing ever go the way I'd like? Why am I cursed to have people discover things mere moments before I'm planning to tell them?

"Larry!" Mom spins on her heel and strides out of the kitchen. My head drops as she rouses him, and I wish I could text Sloane and tell her what I'm about to embark on.

About to tell my folks about my writing career, I'd type out. *And us. And Pittsburgh. Wish me luck!*

And of course, she would. So much luck, with those smiley faces with the hearts for eyes, and then she'd say, *You don't need luck, Logan. Just be your charming self.*

My parents enter the dining-room-kitchen combo, and I turn on the charm. "I've been preparing to talk to you for the past couple of weeks, and I'd appreciate it if you'd let me get all the way to the end before you say anything."

Mom opens her mouth, and I hold up a hand. "No gasping. No crying. No whimpers. No humming." I throw in that last one, though neither of them have ever hummed at me, but I must get it from somewhere.

"Gladys," Dad says. "Sit down. Where are the rest of these crispy treats?" He shuffles into the kitchen behind me.

"Mom, how long until dinner?" I ask.

"Twenty-five minutes." Her voice already sounds

semi-nasally, but I reach way down deep inside myself and grab onto every shred of courage I have.

I'm dying here, in Superior, in my life in its current state. Drowning, with the only life preserver in Sloane Sanders' hand.

"Time enough," I say. "I'll be brief."

Dad returns to the table, and I decide I need a shield between me and them. I open my computer again, the long-term rentals brightening again. There's not enough air in the world to fill my lungs properly.

But I look at my father, whose bright blue eyes mirror mine. He gives me a small nod, and that increases my courage ten-fold. They'll miss me; heck, I'll miss them terribly. But I have enough money, as well as the job flexibility, to fly up here any time I want.

"Mom, I'm in love with my best friend, and she happens to live in Pittsburgh." I turn the computer toward her. "So I need your help picking one where I can live for a month or two while Sloane helps me find a house."

"Logan." Mom speaks and gasps, as I knew she would. Dad simply smiles and takes a huge bite of his crispy treat.

"I don't know if we'll make it." I swallow hard, because I can't live with this truth. Sloane and I are perfect together, even if she doesn't know it yet.

"But I can't date her from here. I have to be there. And since I write books from home, I don't have to live here. I can write and run my publishing business from Pittsburgh."

Dad chokes this time, and a squeak comes from Mom's mouth. I wish I'd thought ahead to take out my phone and film their reactions. Sloane will love them.

This hasn't gone exactly how I planned it, but hardly anything does. My mother is the type of woman who won't put a toe in a pool of water without knowing the exact temperature of it. It hasn't been proven, but I'm pretty sure she's responsible for at least two deaths—from questioning.

Is it warmer than dishwater or not? Are your feet tingling? Is it a good tingle or a tingle that's telling you to get your feet out of the water because it's too cold?

I brace myself for the questions, but she sits there, mute. Sloane won't believe that either, and I smile to myself at being able to tell her face-to-face. I haven't exactly planned the next phase of my life, but I know it involves me choosing one of these long-term rentals, signing the contract, and then packing what I need for a couple of months in Pittsburgh. Really, just clothes, a few things for Titan, and my electronics. They have stores there, after all.

My computer beckons to me, and I turn it back toward me, further shielding myself. I glance over to my father, and his eyes dance with merriment as he crunches into another bite of his marshmallow treat. At least I have his blessing, and if I can't win over my mom, Dad'll do it for me after I leave. It might take him a few days, but it'll get done.

Part of me wails about leaving Superior. I love the lake. I love the slowness of small-town life. I love that I know my neighbors and can easily jog next door and ask for an egg if I'm in the middle of making pasta and run out, but that they leave me alone too.

I tell myself I'm going to love a lot of things about the city of Pittsburgh too. Number one, Sloane lives there, and no matter what I said to her in Atlanta, I'm not ready to give up on us yet. The past couple weeks of silence has solidified that for me.

"How far is it to Pittsburgh?" Mom's voice comes out the way Elmo's would, causing me to remind myself that I've lived here for thirty-four years. Leaving will be a traumatic event no matter what.

"It's a ways, Mom," I say quietly. Sloane says I may speak softly in volume, but there's nothing soft about this powerful voice of mine. She said the day before she found out I'm L.M. Ryan that she loved my "sexy, powerful voice."

"I'm going to take my SUV," I say. "It's winter there too, and I'm taking Titan. I've got it all mapped out, and we're going to stay in a hotel in Chicago along the way." When I get tired of looking at rentals in Pittsburgh, I look at hotels in Chicago. Or dog kennels for big dogs like Titan to ride comfortably in the back of an SUV. Or the weather in Pittsburgh.

I manage to squeak in a couple of hours of writing every day, because I have a self-imposed deadline for my next release date, and I can't just take every day off. I still run, but I dropped out of the cooking class I'd signed up for a few months ago.

I'm not going to be here to see it through to completion, so I saw no point in even starting it. See, the things I begin, I mean to finish—including this thing between me and Sloane.

"It'll take about fourteen hours," I say. "If I don't stop at all, but I've got Titan, so I'm breaking it into two days."

"When are you going?" she asks.

"I haven't worked that out yet," I say. "I haven't found a place yet." I flip the computer around again. "You're a pro at this, Ma. Please help me." Our eyes meet, and she must see something in mine, because her next question dies on her lips.

She looks at the computer, and I wonder when she last did that.

"Sloane?" Mom asks as she peers at my screen. "Does she like you back, Logan?"

"She seems to."

"You said you weren't anything but friends," Dad chimes in, betraying me in the worst way. "All these trips, all these years."

"We haven't been," I say. "Until this year." I shift in my seat but manage not to hum or clear my throat.

"Oh, this one has a two-burner stove, dear." Mom shakes her head, her eyes squinted. "That won't do for you, unless you don't plan to cook in Pittsburgh."

"You're handling this really well," I say.

That causes her to lift her head, surprise entering her own blue eyes. "I only want you to be happy, Logan." She doesn't look away from me as she adds, "You've chosen the oddest places to live."

"I have?"

"This one is three bedrooms." She focuses on the computer again. "What do you need three bedrooms for?"

"For when you and Dad come stay with me," I say without missing a beat.

"Oh, we can't do that."

I knew she'd say that, and I flick a look in Dad's direction. "Sure you can," I say. "I have plenty of money for the tickets."

"No, you don't."

"Mom, yes, I do." It's go-time. Moment of reckoning. Time for the truth to be told. "I write books for a living. Did you guys hear me say that a few minutes ago?"

"I did not," Dad says. "I got stuck on you being in love with Sloane."

"You've never even met her," I say, maybe a little sharper than I mean to.

"Exactly," he says, his eyes flickering with something cold now.

"That's why you'll have to come visit." My voice is smooth and even as I retort without missing a single beat. "Thus, the need for another bedroom. I work from home, so the other one will be an office."

"You and your space issues," Mom murmurs.

"I don't have space issues," I argue. "I like having a living space and a work space. It helps me get my head in the right place to write."

"Novels?" Dad asks.

"Yes." I meet his eyes across the length of the table. It's suddenly too cold in the house, despite Titan's warm body on my feet. "I write romance novels, Dad, under a pen name. I just sold two more books to a major publisher, and I've been supporting myself, paying into a retirement account and everything, for three years now."

Both of my parents gape at me, and Mom flaps at the computer. "What name?"

Heat starts to rise through my chest. "Mom, what are you doing?"

"I'm looking you up."

"How are you going to do that?"

"You don't have a website?" Her hands hover over the keyboard. "Dear, you really should have a website if you're going to be an author."

I blink at her, stunned at the tone of voice she's used with me. It's halfway between saccharine sweet and dry as unbuttered toast. I can't tell if she's teasing or making fun of me, as there's such a fine line between the two.

"L.M. Ryan," I say. "Logan Murphy Ryan."

"Your names out of order," Dad says with a look of incredulity on his face. "Romance novels?" It's not the shaking, near-crying tone Sloane used on me. Nor the one of devil-may-care Hattie had used. It's like he can't believe I'd ever know how to craft a romance novel. Trust me, I've wondered the same thing many times.

"It's fiction, Dad," I say. "You don't actually take your real life experiences and write them all into a book."

"Fiction," he repeats as if he's never read a book before. He has, which is why my sister and I are so educated and well-read. My dad read everywhere we went, from church to the beach to his parents' house for Thanksgiving dinner.

"Yes, fiction." I do clear my throat now. "Sloane has inspired a lot of stories, actually. I think—"

"Logan Ryan Murphy," Mom yelps. "These books have bestseller flags."

I manage to keep my smile hidden. "I'm doing pretty well," I say. "So please, please come to Pittsburgh in a month or so and meet Sloane."

"Does she love you too?" Mom asks, finally closing my computer.

As much as it pains me to speak the truth, I have to. "I'm not sure," I say slowly. "That's why I have to go there. We talked about it—me moving there—in Belize, but we... left things in a weird place."

I left things between us in a weird place. Me. Then, when I finally got back to Superior and picked up Titan and made it home, I was too tired to text her back. So much had happened on the flight and drive home, all of it inside me.

The following day, I'd felt more like myself, and while I'd been thrilled she'd texted me, it felt friendly. Like what she'd have done last year, when we were still just friends. Since that isn't what I want, I'd texted her back briefly and left it there.

She hasn't messaged or called me since, and every day, another part of me dies a little bit more.

"Mom, I need help with the rentals."

She smiles and shakes her head. She reaches her hand across the space between us and covers mine with it. "No, you don't. You need to stop procrastinating, get home and pack your bag, and go."

"You make it sound so easy," I grumble. "Are you kicking me out before dinner?"

"If that's what it takes." She stands and heads into the kitchen. "I honestly don't know how you're still here. When you love a person, you'll do anything to be with them."

"Yeah," I mutter as I open my machine again. The rentals blare back to life. *Just pick one.* "I know."

* * *

The next Wednesday finds me zipping closed my backpack after putting my laptop inside. My house smells like lemon furniture polish, because that's what my house-keepers use on Tuesday afternoons to swipe away all the dust.

Titan raises his head from where he's laying on the bed, and I say, "Come on, bud. Today's the day. Road trip."

He cocks his head, because he doesn't exactly know those words. Our longest road trips up to this point have been the four miles to my parents' house. Then back. Sometimes we go to the lakes in the region, but it's winter and has been very cold for months. I'm not sure how long dogs can remember things, but I'm certain if I've ever used those words to describe one of our days at the lake, it's been long enough for him to forget.

"You can ride up front for a little while, okay?" I lift my pack and leave my bedroom. I've made my bed, done all my laundry, and my dishwasher hums. I'm not going to be back for eight weeks—the amount of time I signed on the rental contract for a three-bedroom, two-bathroom house in a suburb of Pittsburgh.

It has a little yard, not that it matters. The management company said it's pretty socked in with snow there, and I'd assured the woman I spoke with that I'm used to the weather. Once I'd told her where I was coming from, she said, "Oh, sure. Then you have all the cold weather gear."

I'd told her I did, and I lift the duffle bag full of it as I pass the coat closet in the hall. Both of those bags get loaded in the backseat of my SUV, where I've folded down two-thirds of the seat to make more cargo space. I return to the house to get my suitcases. I've packed two, and they both fit in the extra space I've created, one behind the other. Titan's kennel is anchored by the seat that's still up and one of my suitcases, and I head inside to get his bag.

Leashes, food, dental chews, and some toys. I can buy more when I get there, but this should be enough for the trip and a few days. He's waiting for me in the living room now, and I say, "Come on, friend," and he trots toward me. "We're getting in the car. In the car." I don't know why people always raise their voice and repeat themselves with dogs, but I know when I don't, Titan thinks he can run freely up and down the street.

I open the front door again, twist the lock, and check my pockets for my keys, wallet, and phone. All set, I let Titan out, calling after him, "In the car!" before I pull the door shut and use the keypad to engage the deadbolt.

I turn around, inhale deeply, and take that first step toward Pittsburgh.

Chapter Twenty-Two
Sloane

The real estate office where I work must own stock in Stark White Wall Paint because it's all we have. It makes everything glaring, and on a day like today, where I have a headache and no showings, I feel trapped. The walls are literally closing in on me, ready to smash me with clapboard white hands.

I imagine how stained they'd be then, and pretend to look at something interesting on my computer screen. I can't. There is nothing interesting about sifting through the MLS listings, trying to find the perfect house for a client when I've already done it.

And lost it.

I put my head in my arms, relishing in the cool grayness created by blocking the sunshine on the white faces all around me. The sunshine, however, is very deceiving. I've lived here long enough to know that I need two scarves when the sky is as blue as it is today. The sun isn't warm; it means there's no cloud cover, and thus no heat trapped beneath them.

I just want to go home, and I lift my head to check the time. Ten-thirty. How can that be? I've been here for an hour and a half? No way. It feels like one and a half years.

I've given up counting the silence between me and Logan in hours. There are too many, and it brings me to tears every time I let the thought linger for longer than a few seconds. I've reverted to days, which are up to nineteen.

My phone sits on my desk, silent. I enter into a battle of wills with it, but the device can't blink, so I'm going to lose. I can stop myself from looking at it, though, and I do that intensely for a few minutes, even going so far as to open my email.

Then I accidentally look down, and my eyes catch on my phone. Shoot. Two for the cellphone. Zero for me. After another few minutes of feigned working, I pick it up. Perhaps I left it on silent after I woke up this morning and painted on my perfect real estate agent face. That's why I haven't heard it chiming out all of my notifications. Friends, family, co-workers, clients. I should have easily a dozen texts by now.

I have zero.

A frown tugs at my eyebrows, and my thumbs automatically move into my texting app. Logan's string is pinned to the top, and I flick my fingers down several times, really getting the conversation moving backward through time quite quickly.

It settles to a stop, and I scroll slowly to find the date timestamped above one of the messages. January third. I have no idea what we talked about on January third, but it floods back into my mind with only one sentence.

Salmon is the superior fish for sure, Logan had told me. From there, we'd talked about our favorite foods, and Logan had sent me link after link for possible restaurants in the Florida Keys, where we were meant to vacation this year.

Reading through his texts, I feel so...happy. It oozes out of our playful back-and-forth, and never once did I think he liked me for more than a friend when these texts were originally sent.

Now that I'm reading back through them, I start to see something different. At one point, he asks me if I have any new swimming suits this year, to which I told him I always buy a fresh crop of swimwear for every trip.

Oh, that's right, he'd said. *Anything like that lime green one last year?* He'd sent the face emoji that's panting with that one, and I remember laughing at it.

I'm not wearing lime green again. Lesson learned.

Yeah, go with something red or pink, he told me. And I had. I hadn't thought much of it, because of course a dark blonde with my skin coloring shouldn't wear lime green. When you're practically an albino, darker colors are always better. It's no small wonder that the bulk of my clothes are black or navy blue, with some pops of color in the blouses and scarves I choose to wear.

I reach the end of memory lane with the sad texts post-Belize and toss my phone back to my desk. One of my clients—an adorably cute couple who've outgrown their current home—needs me to find them a new crop of houses to look at. We found their dream house last week and put in an offer that was then turned down.

The homeowner had chosen someone else, and as the wife had started to weep, I'd wanted to grab her by the shoulders and tell her to buck up. Life doesn't always go your way, and you can't cry over it. It's a house. In Pittsburgh.

It's not like they won't have one. They do—a nice one too. I know, because I listed it for sale right after I returned from Belize. We still don't have an offer, but I had four people through it this week already, and I'm expecting a call from one of the showing agents this morning.

Though I'm only thirty-one years old, I've learned that for some people, life does always go well. For Regina Hinkenklaus, it has. She gets chosen for things, including the high school cheer squad, college scholarships, and any houses she puts offers in on. In my opinion, she's lost the Last Name Lottery, but with everything else, she's batting a thousand.

Thus, the tears.

Guaranteed she hasn't spent nineteen days pining after a man who lives in another state and whom she won't see again for another three hundred and thirty days, if at all.

Those last three words in my thoughts make my breath catch. *If at all.*

I yank open my desk drawer and pull out my purse. I can search the MLS from home, and I don't have to keep office hours here at the agency. My phone rings, saving me from sprinting from the building, and I lift it to see Rose's name there.

Guilt assaults me as I swipe the call away. I can't help it, and I can say I was driving or with a client. It won't be the first time, and Rose knows what kind of job I work. I've got my coat on and am straightening my collar when she calls again.

Sighing, I dig deep for an internal reserve of patience. We've chosen the linens for her wedding luncheon, and she's found a florist to do the flowers. She's still working on a caterer, but she and Spencer signed a contract for a venue—a lovely antique barn outside the city that comes with misters and fans for the early August weather.

On the last ring, I tap the icon to answer. "I don't have much time," I say.

"That's fine." She too sounds winded. "I'm just wondering what you're doing tonight."

Part of me wants to make up an imaginary date with my imaginary boyfriend, but Lean Cuisine doesn't sound like a sexy name for my ripped, struts-around-the-house-without-his-shirt-on boyfriend.

I scoff while my traitorous mind conjures up an image of Logan. He doesn't strut, but he doesn't wear a shirt very often either. *While you're on vacation*, I remind myself. I barely know him as a real person, which makes this funk I've fallen into absolutely ridiculous.

"Nothing," I say. "Why? Did you want to go to Girls' Night at Tiny's?" My voice is far too hopeful to go unnoticed, but Rose plows onward.

"No, not Tiny's. I'm meeting a caterer after work to do a testing."

"Okay." Then why did she call and ask me what I'm doing tonight?

"Gotta go."

"Rose."

But she's gone, the call silent on her end of the line. I pull my phone away from my ear and gape at it. "What in the world?" This engagement has her acting strange, and I vow that next time she calls, I won't answer. For at least twenty-four hours. Then she won't ask me nonsensical questions and leave me hanging.

The real estate office reminds me of the kind of place people go after they die. Everything is staged just-so, with fake flowers on all the credenzas-not-counters. All the desks sit at right angles, making grids for the walkways between them. Windows make up the whole front wall of the office, and in the spring and summer, the sunlight is so powerful we have to cover them with blinds. In the winter, they only remind us of how gray everything is.

We have gift baskets made of fake recycled barn wood that once held loaves of bread and fancy chocolate covered pretzels, but that now boast pens. Everyone that walks in pauses for a moment, wondering if it's a real place or if they've gone to heaven. The only difference is where heaven has those pearly gates, we have a sign-in book.

I'm almost past that when my boss says, "Sloane."

I turn back to him, sure I can blow him off with a well-placed sentence about needing to meet a client. One look at his face, however, and my heart sinks into my heels. Therol White wears navy slacks that fit him like a glove, a brown belt around his trim waist, and a pale yellow shirt tucked into both. His tie is navy and silver, and his round glasses and bald head complete the perfect picture of power player.

"I need you for a minute," he says.

Those six words can be promising or excruciating, and as I click my way back to his office, I have a guess at which they'll be today. When he smiles quickly and then closes the door behind me, I know I'm not sneaking out anywhere. If I had a client, Therol would have me reschedule.

"What's going on?" I ask, suddenly nervous. I don't have work hours; as long as I bring in my monthly quota for the agency, I'm fine.

"I need your help with the Glyphs." He doesn't sit behind his desk, but in front of it, where the guest chairs are. "They're driving me crazy, and I need your eyes." He looks up at me as I sink into the chair beside him.

His laptop is open to the agent-facing MLS, and he looks at me hopefully. Internally, I sigh. Externally, I dig into my purse and pull out a pad of paper with the pen stuck into the wire along the top. A sense of excitement —or at least not complete misery—accompanies the motion.

I click the pen. "Give me the specs, and then tell me their history."

He starts talking, and I jot down what I need. They are particular clients, because they have millions to spend. Only certain neighborhoods interest them, and after only ten minutes of explanation, I understand why he's struggling to find somewhere for them.

"Send me their file," I say once he finishes talking. "Maybe there's nothing for them right now, but we can set up a filtering flag system." I make a note in my little booklet. "I can also expand the search to beyond Pittsburgh."

Therol nods. "Will you spend a little time today looking through the ones I've marked in their file?"

"Yep."

"And...they want to meet this afternoon with the prospects. Can you come with me?"

With my heart somewhere in my right leg as it slides downward again, I say, "Yep," as cheerfully as I can, which is about the enthusiasm level of a bush.

"Perfect," he says. "Thanks, Sloane."

"Yep," I say for the third time, and before it becomes the only word I can say, I leave his office.

By the time I pull into my driveway and wait for the garage door to lift, it's dark. I spent all day on Therol's clients, and my shoulders are tense in a way I haven't felt in weeks. Months, even.

The front of my house always makes it look like no one's home. There's a porch between two windows, and then the garage, but they belong to a formal living room and an office. I have lamps in both, and any movement on the front porch, sidewalks, or driveway makes the lamps burst to life.

My front door sits back between the two halves of the house, and I can't see it from my perspective right now. I don't think I see any packages though, and that's a relief. Then I can go inside, pour myself a big glass of wine, and cry myself to sleep. Again.

Logan still hasn't called or texted, and a heady, unbearable desperation builds beneath my tongue. Someone has to say something.

After I ease into the garage, I reach to close the door with the button in my car. I never get out after dark with the door yawning open for the world to see. Anyone could rush out of the bushes along the front of my house, ambushing me. A single woman needs to have some safety precautions in place.

I sit in my warm car as the door lowers and reach for my phone. I have to text Logan tonight. One of us will have to break the silence, and I'm fine if it's me. He's bounced the ball so far into my court that my *I-made-it-home* text wasn't strong enough.

Let's see what else I can do.

Hey, Logan, I start out. I stop there, because I'm not sure if I'm addressing it right. "No," I murmur, my brain working overtime now. "You are." Logan is my boyfriend, the man I need to get to know.

Murph is my vacation buddy. My best friend. The travel version of the man I need to get to know.

I hate that there's this silence between us, so I'm breaking it. I don't want to go to Florida next year. I want to go to the Caribbean. The Cayman Islands again, or St. Thomas or St. Lucia or one of the other saints. I don't actually know how many there are.

And I want to go with you, as my boyfriend.

I don't think it matters if I liked you because you liked me first. I don't think we have to start in the same place or be in the same place all the time. The scale is a slider, Logan, and maybe you're just ahead of me right now.

But I play a great catch-up game, and I want us to try. I need us to try.

Please call me when you can. I miss the sound of your voice.

I sit in my car and weep, the tears tracking down my face slowly. There's so much more I want to tell him— about today's complete waste of a day at work, about

Rose's wedding plans, about the perfect rentals I found for him.

I can't do that if he won't talk to me. This text is me chucking the ball back to him, and I can't honestly predict what will happen if he refuses to catch it. What if he doesn't call?

My heart shrivels at the very thought, and I hesitate to send the text. Right now, we're just in a stalemate. I can invent any number of endings, but we're *not* to the end yet. If I send this text, and he doesn't respond, everything is over.

Pulse pounding, mind spinning, my thumb hovers over the arrow that will send the message to him. Seconds tick by, and I'm not sure what to do. Staying where we are isn't healthy or ideal. Accepting that we're done and over is absolutely unacceptable.

"So if he doesn't answer," I muse. "You'll get on a plane and go talk to him face-to-face." With that as my answer, I manage to send the text. Because if he doesn't answer, I now have a plan for the next step.

I know he won't respond instantly, though he has in the past. We're not who we were before Belize, and with a text as long and as meaningful as I've just sent, he'll read it a few times before he formulates a response.

I tuck my phone into my purse and get out of the SUV. My garage is big enough for two cars, but it's just me here, so the other half is littered with my yard care tools, a stand-up chest freezer that only holds frozen pizzas and popsicles, and cases and cases of water. Bypassing it all, I take the three cement steps to my house and enter it.

The air is scented with browned meat and oregano, garlic and tomatoes. I did not put anything in my slow cooker this morning.

A dog barks once. I do not own a dog.

A man with windswept blond hair and a black apron tied around his runner's waist turns toward me. Logan smiles, his mouth full of straight, white teeth, and says, "It took you a few minutes to come inside."

I have no idea what's happening. His dog rushes toward me, his face happy and eager to be my new best friend.

Logan is cooking. In my kitchen. Logan is cooking in my kitchen.

I don't even have time or brain capacity to wonder if he's seen my text yet. I simply burst into tears and bury my face in both of my hands.

Chapter Twenty-Three
Sloane

"**S**loane, come on," Logan calls from the other side of the bedroom door. "I don't care about your raccoon eyes." Through the wood, I can't tell if he's irritated or genuine. I scrub at my face with the makeup remover wipe, still weeping tracks of tears down my face.

As I'd felt the water in my hands standing in the kitchen, I'd been mortified that seeing him had caused such a strong reaction. My mind had short-circuited to my makeup melting off my face, and I'd run into my bedroom.

Logan's been trying to get me to come out for ten minutes now.

"Dinner's ready," he says. "You like your food hot."

I finally get the last of my face cleaned up, and I look at myself in the mirror. My hair is clipped back professionally, and I reach to let it down. With it falling in waves across my shoulders and down my back, and now that I'm makeup-less, I feel more like myself. I've already changed out of my stupid heels, skirt, and blouse, and I'm wearing a pair of puddle sweats and a tee-shirt from Oahu that proudly broadcasts my once-upon-a-time visit to the pineapple plantation.

This is who I am, and I'm not going to hide it from Logan. I've no reason to wear a swimming suit right now, and if he hadn't been standing in my kitchen, this is exactly what I would've done.

"Sloane," he tries again.

I leave my bathroom and head for the door. Every step I take makes me feel strong and sure and sexy, and when I pull open the door, Logan's eyes lift immediately to meet mine. We simply look at one another, each moment being marked in my memory as significant. I'm not sure why, but these types of things are generally only seen in hindsight.

His gaze leaves mine to slide down to my bare feet and back. "Wow," he says, his mouth barely moving.

I have no idea what that means. Part of me gets fired up, ready for a fight. The other part prays it's a compliment.

I gesture to the sweats and vacation tee. "This is what I do after work," I say. "I change out of my oppressive clothes and into something that has no form. That doesn't expect me to be an hourglass. That's comfortable."

"You look great," he says.

I can't tell if he's joking, and I tell myself of course he isn't. Logan doesn't just hand out cheap compliments.

"Why are you here?" I ask, when I want to ask if he got my text or not. He's not holding his phone, and he wasn't when he turned to face me from the stove either.

His expression sobers, though his eyes still dance with light.

"How did you get into my house?" I ask without waiting for him to answer the first question.

His lips tip up into a half-smile, and he folds his arms. "Are you done?"

"No." I don't try to move past him and into the hall-way, and he's not trying to come into my bedroom. "What did you make for dinner? Did you get my text? How long have you been in Pittsburgh? Will you be crashing in my guest room tonight?"

I conveniently buried the one about my text in the middle, and when I finally run out of air, Logan starts to laugh. But I don't want to be laughed at. All of those were very serious questions, and I fold my arms, cock my hip, and glare.

When he doesn't stop, I brush by him and go into the kitchen. I shouldn't ruin this. He's here! All I've wanted was to hear his voice and be near him, and now he's here and I'm walking away.

"Sloane," he says from behind me. In the living room, his dog lays on my couch, and Titan lifts his head as we return to the main body of the house. Logan is a very neat cook, and my house looks exactly as I left it this morning, except there's now two plates of chicken over wild rice pilaf and some sort of sauce. Gobs and gobs of mushrooms.

It's exactly what I want to eat, and it's obvious Logan has thought of me while making it.

"I'm here because I can't stand the silence between us either."

I pause, my heart suddenly galloping like a whole herd of wild horses. He got the text. Two questions answered.

"I got into the house using the garage code, which Rose provided for me. She said you didn't have any plans tonight, and I figured if I could deliver on one of your dreams, you'd take me back."

I turn in a slow circle to face him. He indicates the plated food. "It's chicken Marsala, modified. Double the mushrooms." His eyes do that dancing thing I love so much. "I've been in Pittsburgh for about two hours, and no, I'm not crashing here tonight. I have a long-term rental for the next couple of months."

The air rushes out of my lungs, brushing by my lips as I gasp. Logan steps closer, very nearly into me, as he picks up his phone. "I got your text, and I agree. One of the saints sounds way better than Florida."

A fresh set of tears blurs him, but not enough that I don't see that gorgeous smile.

"And yes, I want us to go as a couple, not a couple of friends. I have missed *everything* about you, from your voice, to your eyes, to the way you wear oversized tee-shirts." He keeps that mega-watt smile in place, and I love it so much. "I came, because I miss the sound of your voice too. I came, because I was dying in Superior, and the only person who can revive me is here in Pittsburgh. I came, because I'm in love with you, and I need us to try too."

His chest rises and falls quickly now, like he's been out running with Titan. "That's it," he says. "I'm done. You can talk now."

I step closer to him, absorbing the warmth from his body. Taking his phone, I drop it into one of my oversized pockets. I put one hand on his arm, the spot where our skin meets the temperature of hot lava.

"I'd have vacuumed up your Cheetos crumbs," he whispers. "If there were any here. I didn't see any, and I didn't want to snoop too much."

I still don't say anything, but my hand moves up his chest inch by inch.

"Are you going to say something?" he asks.

I shake my head. "I don't want to talk." My voice sounds like a frog compared to his.

His eyebrows go up. "No?"

Another shake of my head. I lean fully into him, and he has to steady me with his hands on my waist so we both don't topple to the ground. I tip my head back and let my eyes drift closed. "No. I want you to kiss me."

His breath washes over my face in the next moment, but his lips don't meet mine. Anticipation builds between us, soaring up to the ceiling, where it holds its breath. The whole house feels like someone has pressed pause, and the only way to get life moving again is for us to kiss.

"It's okay that we're not in the same place on the slider," he whispers. "As long as we're on the same page in what we want."

"We are," I breathe. Him. I want him. I'm pretty sure he wants me.

"Mm." He touches his mouth to mine finally, seeking, exploring.

Fireworks pop along my lips, and I thread my fingers through his hair to hold him close. He kisses me carefully for only a moment, and then he speeds things up and takes them deeper. I can't get close enough to him, and I stand in my kitchen with dinner ready and growing cold and kiss him, kiss him, kiss him.

There's nothing else I want to do, and we continue on like we'll both die if our lips aren't touching the other's. The seconds and minutes pass, and maybe a whole hour. I don't know. I know Logan's mouth is better than any margarita or daiquiri I've ever had. I know the heat of his body warms me perfectly. I know his hands in my hair and down my back send shivers through me in the very best way possible.

He finally breaks our connection, only to press his forehead to mine. We breathe in together, and that definitely feels like we're on the same page.

"What was that 'hm' right before you kissed me?" I whisper.

"It was me agreeing that we're on the same page."

I open my eyes, pull back, and meet his. "You've got a long-term rental?"

"Yes, ma'am." He holds onto my hips but steps back. "So I can see you after work, before work, on weekends, whenever."

"We can get to know each other as real people and not the vacation versions of ourselves."

"Mm."

I bite back the question about whether he might not like the non-vacation Sloane. He's already told me he loves me.

I came, because I'm in love with you. I haven't said it back, because I'm not sure I'm in love with Logan. I don't think it'll take too much longer for me to know, but I want to be responsible about this relationship. I want to make sure I love him because I love him, not because he loved me first.

I nod and say, "Okay." I glance over to the chicken dinners on the counter. "And the Cheetos need to be vacuumed out of my SUV, not my house." My attention swings back to him, my smile kicking into high gear.

Logan chuckles, doesn't say he'll get right on that, but that's okay. Because he pulls me close and kisses me again.

Chapter Twenty-Four
Logan

I pull up to the little red brick house on Midnight Street, where the only thing I dislike about it is the street name. Some people probably find it charming. I simply find it a bit kitschy.

But the house at 512 Midnight Street is absolutely perfect for me.

"Are you coming?" Sloane asks from halfway up the sidewalk. "It's freezing, and we only get twenty minutes." She gestures me forward impatiently, but I think the outside view of a house speaks volumes. It's like a book cover—they tell a thousand stories before a reader even cracks the spine on the novel.

I can look at the photos online again, but I pull out my phone and snap a picture of the house. Then I can send it to my parents and Hattie to show them where I'm going to be permanently living in Pittsburgh.

I hope. Maybe. *Please*, I think as I hurry after Sloane. She's managed to get me a second showing of this house, but I don't really need to walk through it again now that I've seen the house from the curb.

"I want to offer," I say as I join her inside the home.

She rotates toward me, but her gaze is on the ceiling. "These beams really are amazing."

"I think you're so sexy in that coat." I grin, because I'm pretty sure she's gone into show-agent mode and hasn't actually heard me. She's wearing a bright red peacoat, and it matches her lips so perfectly, I want to kiss her just to make her mouth a different color.

Her honeyed blonde hair spills over the collar of the coat as she steps past me in a pair of matte-black heels. "New paint. Great layout."

I chuckle and follow her past the office that fills the front room of the house. It has great light and a view of the jogging path across the street. Titan can sit in the bay window and bark at all the other dogs as they go by, and we can head out the front door and begin our run in mere seconds.

The kitchen and living room sit at the back of the house, with a full bathroom off the kitchen and a bedroom behind it. My master suite is in the last corner of the house, complete with another bathroom. Upstairs are two more bedrooms and another bath. This house is technically larger than I need or even want, but it ticks every other box to perfection.

Plus, I can just *feel* like this is where I belong. I let Sloane lead me around like I haven't been here before, and nineteen minutes later, I repeat myself. "I want to make an offer."

Her mouth perks up. "Good. Great. I'll get it written up when I get back to the office." She pulls open the front door and exits the home. "I think we should go in right at asking. They don't have any other offers yet, and it's priced exactly on the market. A lowball offer might upset them, and there's no need to go higher if we don't have to."

"Great," I say. She's the professional, not me. "When will we know?"

"I'll give them twenty-four hours to accept, decline, or counter."

Twenty-four hours. I turn back to the house as I round my SUV to get behind the wheel. Once I do, I look over to Sloane in my passenger seat. "I really hope I get it."

She covers my hand with hers. "Don't worry, Logan," she says with more confidence than I've ever heard from her. "I'm not going to let you lose this house."

I hope she's right, because my long-term rental is up in two weeks, and I need to have something more permanent here. I can extend the contract at the house where I live now, but I'd like an end-game in sight.

Things between Sloane and I are good. Great, even. I've yet to vacuum up any crumbs, but we get together every evening after work. I know she lets her clothes sit in the dryer for days before folding them, and I know she still won't eat red onions. She adores Titan and has joked about getting into running shape so she can come jogging with me and my dog.

I know it annoys her when I show up at her house without calling or texting first, and I know she kicks her shoes off the moment she enters the house. I offered to buy her a rack to put beside her back door, but she declined. She goes around on Sunday mornings and puts her shoes away, ready for the upcoming week. Her and her routines, which make me smile when I think about them.

I know I love her a little bit more each day, and I know we belong together, and I just know she's going to get me this house.

She hasn't told me she loves me yet, but I don't have to hear it in words. Don't get me wrong, I want to hear her say it. She will when she's ready.

I see it in the way she looks at me when I'm reading on her couch at night.

I smell it in the way she stops by my house in the morning with my favorite coffee and a lemon poppyseed muffin top.

I taste it in the way she kisses me, holding onto my collar as I stand at her front door, ready to leave.

I hear it in the way she says, "Don't go, Logan," right before she kisses me again.

I feel it in the way she holds my hand, smiles at me, texts me, and says things like, "When we're married, we won't have those tacky mints at our reception, okay?"

In those simple moments, I simply smile to myself and agree with her.

"Did you want me to drop you at the agency to get your car now?" I glance over to her. "Or should we get it after dinner?"

She's got her head leaned back against the head rest, and she turns to look at me. She wears the weight of the world on her shoulders sometimes, especially when it comes to her sisters and her mother. I've met them all now, but her dad isn't in the picture at all yet.

"Let's just go." She smiles sleepily, and I reach over and take her hand.

After lifting it to my lips, I say, "Okay," in a quiet voice. We don't talk on the way to the restaurant, which is fine with me, because my heartbeat is currently trying to flee my body like it's robbed a bank and needs to get to the getaway car.

Sloane's birthday is tomorrow, but her mother has planned a big birthday dinner for her. I guess it was done and set before I moved to Pittsburgh, and Sloane doesn't want to upset anyone. Thus, we're going to dinner to celebrate her birthday tonight.

The parking lot at her favorite place—Noble's Pizza Pie—doesn't look too full yet. I manage to find a spot between a giant black SUV and a tiny electric blue hatchback and put my vehicle in park.

"So." I swallow, the walls of my throat sticking together. "The big three-two tomorrow."

She grins at me, that light suddenly back in her eyes. "Yep."

"Happy birthday, Sloany." I lean across the console and kiss her, glad when she meets me halfway. I can honestly stay in this car all night, kissing her and making sure she knows how much I love her and want to be with her. Instead, I pull away after only a few strokes and say, "I love you."

She keeps her eyes closed, sends her tongue across the slit between her lips, and says, "I love you too, Logan."

I suck in a breath and pull back. Sloane's eyes come open. I search her face, finding the truth of her words shining in those pretty blue eyes. I laugh and try to match my mouth to hers again.

"Stop it." She giggles too and pushes against my chest futilely.

"You love me," I tease. "You love me *sooo* much."

"Yeah." She grins and grins, then sends her face straight back to sober. "What are you gonna do about it?"

I don't buy her tough woman act for even half a second. "Sounds like we better start talking about marriage a little more than we have."

Anxiety floods her eyes now, but I take her face in my hands. "Sweetheart, there's nothing to be worried about. I'm not Leon, remember?"

"No, I know." Her eyes fall closed in a slow blink. "It's just... I thought we'd date a while just to make sure."

"We will."

She searches my face now. "But you just said—"

"That we should start *talking* about it more," I say. "That doesn't mean I'm going to propose tomorrow or anything."

"I don't want you to propose on my birthday."

"I just said I wasn't going to." She's freaking out already, and I don't know how to make her stop. "Sloane, look at me."

She docs, but her gaze flits away just as fast. Maybe the envelope I have in the holder of my door isn't a good idea. *It is*, I tell myself.

"Let's go in," I say. "It's your birthday dinner, and I have a present for you." We get out and go into the pizza parlor. It's one of those cool, hip places that makes me feel like maybe I've wandered into the wrong spot. I'm neither cool nor hip, but I do love their funky combinations of flavors here.

The floor is all white tile, with colorful pop art on the walls. Each table has been assigned an artist, and the table-tops boast their paintings or drawings from beneath a thick sheet of glass. The napkin dispensers have been painted bright colors like pink, teal, and violet, and I always feel like I might be putting something in my mouth I don't want to.

It's always delicious, though, and Sloane absolutely loves the vibe of Noble's. We get a table in the corner with a rare white napkin dispenser and put in our drink orders.

Sloane nods to the envelope in my hand, and I quickly slide it under my leg. "What's that?"

"It's..." I can't get the last word out. *Nothing* would be a lie, and Sloane's eyebrows go up. "I have some news," I say instead.

The eyebrows stretch higher. "I am finally going to go public as L.M. Ryan."

"Logan." She gasps and covers her mouth with one hand. "Really?" she asks from behind it.

"Really." I nod and look down at the Degas dancers in front of me. They wear ballet clothes and stretch their arms and legs in preparation for a lesson. "I signed up for a huge reader event and signing." I'm the one who can't quite hold Sloane's gaze now. My eyes seem to flit everywhere, taking in the low-hanging lights above the table next to us and how the couple there has ordered three pizzas for two people.

My pulse riots again as I think of Sloane in her bathing suit one day and then lining up to get some books signed the next.

"There's a problem, though," I say, having rehearsed this a thousand times in my head. A few times in the mirror too. I may be spontaneous, but I don't like going into a situation with Sloane without some plan, even if it is sketchy.

"A problem?"

"It's at the same time as our mid-winter trip."

Sloane falls back in her chair like my words have

bowled her over. She blinks rapidly as pure shock rolls across her face. "The same time? Why did you pick that one?"

I'm giddy with excitement, and I lift the envelope and push it across the table to her. "I had to change the location of our trip, and I added my signing to the beginning of it. Then, we can hit the beach and relax for days and days."

She looks at the envelope like it'll grow fangs and bite her if she reaches for it. "What is this?"

"It's part our mid-winter trip, and part your birthday present. I had to change the details, so I'm paying for the whole thing."

"Logan, you can't—"

"I can," I say over her. "It's a business trip now."

"That is not true."

"My flight will be paid for by my business, and at least two of the nights." I cover the envelope with two hands. "Sloane, this is a gift for your birthday. I need you to just accept it." I lift my eyebrows now, asking her if she'll do that.

She seems like she's going to say no, and I honestly hadn't planned for that. If I'd bought her some jewelry or a gift card for Shoe City, she'd take that and run. This should be no different.

"The mid-winter trip is—"

"Going to change," I say, interrupting her again. "Sloane, it's never going to be fifty-fifty the way it was before. We're together now. One hundred percent. Right?"

"Right." She doesn't seem thrilled by this idea, but I am. *I* want to take her on luxurious beach vacations, hold her at night, and drift out to sea with her, both of us floating on our backs and letting the waves undulate around us. I want to give her the world. Every dream she's ever had, I want to make come true. This is just the first of what I hope to be many.

I pull my hands back and say, "If you can agree to that, you can open it and see where we'll be going."

Curiosity pricks her expression, and her fingers twitch toward the nondescript envelope. After a few seconds of some internal battle, she picks it up. "I was excited about St. Lucia," she says in her real estate agent voice.

"We'll go there," I promise her. "Just not next year." I nod and grin, encouraging her. "Go on. Open it."

She does, easily untucking the flap from the back of the envelope. It holds a single sheet of paper to a fancy, all-inclusive resort. I wonder how long it'll take her to see the destination. Her eyes start to scan left-right, left-right.

One...two...three...four...

She shrieks and presses the paper to her chest with both hands. Her eyes are the brightest I've ever seen, and I start to laugh as she stands up and dances around the table, more yipping coming from her mouth.

I don't even care that she's attracting the attention of

every single person in this place. I wanted her to be happy, and she's definitely that.

"Logan!" She drops into my lap and kisses me. "I've always wanted to go here. Thank you, thank you, thank you."

There's too much kissing happening for a public place, but I don't stop her. A cleared throat and a man saying, "You guys need to cool it. We're a family-friendly place," does, and Sloane pops right up off my lap.

"Yes, sir," she says, saluting him with the paper. "Sorry, sir." She returns to her seat, and with the shiniest eyes I've ever seen her wear, she says, "I love you, Logan. This is going to be so great." She tucks the paper back into the envelope and sighs at it.

I simply reach for her hands and hold both of them in mine. "Yeah, I think so too."

Chapter Twenty-Five
Sloane - 11 months later

"Did you see that guy?" I laugh as I watch the man saunter down the beach in a swimming suit that barely covers his cheeks. "I had no idea the men in Australia wore swimming suits like that."

Logan doesn't answer, which isn't that surprising. He's been working nonstop for the three days we've been in Sydney, but today is finally the first day of our annual midwinter trip. I can't believe that the past eleven months have passed already, or that Logan and I are standing at the back windows of the lobby in one of the most prestigious luxury resorts on the Gold Coast of Australia.

Our rooms aren't quite ready yet, and I lift my hand to my mouth to chew on my fingernail.

"I've overpacked, clearly," Logan finally says. He swings his attention to me, and I see the exhaustion lines around his eyes.

"Our rooms will be ready any second," I tell him as I lace my arm through his. "I'm sure of it."

"I just need a nap today," he says with a yawn. "And we've already agreed on our downtime day being tomorrow."

"Yep." We'll just hang out on the beach or by the pool all day, doing nothing. Excursions and all the wonder and glory Australia has to offer will start the day after that.

This trip is a little longer than our previous ones have been. One, Logan had to work for three days of it, and he'd been brilliant at the reader event. The line at his table had been long for hours, and he'd chatted with fans and signed every book he'd had shipped to the convention center.

Not a single person had given him any grief for his Y chromosome, and he'd been so happy and animated after the signing each day. I love him for how hard he works and for how dedicated he is to his craft—and his fans.

But now, we both need some downtime. I start to check over my shoulder to see if anyone is coming our way just as a woman says, "Mister Murphy? I need to talk to you for a moment."

Logan and I both turn toward her, and my eyes meet hers. She gives an imperceptible nod, her hands worrying about a single folder in her hand. She's dressed in a cool blue skirt and a white top, the uniform for this resort, and there should be two folders. One for each room. One for each of us.

Logan doesn't seem to notice, and I tuck my smile away before it shows too broadly.

"What is it?" he asks. "Are the rooms ready?"

The woman—her name is Candice—glances at me. "I'm so sorry," she says in her Australian accent. She genuinely sounds sorry too. "But I only have one room available."

A shocked grunt comes out of Logan's mouth, and it's like that has stolen all of his words, because he says nothing else.

"That can't be right," I supply for him. "We had two rooms. I saw the booking."

"Yes," she says carefully. "But somehow they got merged in our system."

"There's hundreds of rooms here," he says. "Are you fully booked?"

"Just for the level of room you purchased, sir," she says. "I have plenty of rooms on the backside of the resort if you'd like—"

"No," I say, and I step in front of Logan. His hands hang forcefully at his side, his fingers clenched into fists. I take them into mine and try to work them loose. "Logan, I want the oceanfront room."

"There's just the one of those left." The woman gives a small cough. "It has a big bed, and I can send up as many pillows as you'd like. There's a couch as well, with a pull-out bed."

I raise my eyebrows, but Logan doesn't find this as

285

amusing as I do. I lean closer to him. "We've shared a bed before. You like holding me at night."

His eyes search mine, sudden understanding lighting them. "You—I do. We have."

"Then why pay for two rooms?" I fiddle with the button on his polo shirt, hoping my flirting comes across the right way. Playful and fun, while also clearly stating that I want to share a room with him again.

He clears his throat and looks past me. "All right," he says. "Is the room ready?"

"Yes, sir." The woman turns and takes a step away. "I just need you to sign something, and I'll go over the resort with you." Instead of returning to the check-in counter, she takes a seat at a table with four cushy chairs around it. They're also blue, with peach-and-white-colored pillows as accents. Very beachy.

"Would you like a drink?" A waiter places a napkin on the table, one for me and one for Logan.

"Yes," I say. "I want something fun and fruity, without too much alcohol."

"We have one called a Runaway," he says. "To go with the name of the beach. It's pineapple, mango, and lime, with just an ounce of vodka."

"Yes, that." I look at Logan, and he surprises me by saying, "Two of those, please."

He doesn't even really like frou-frou fruity drinks. But we're not our regular selves anymore. I've forgotten already, because of the book signing where he had to be the charming, personable author he is.

He claims to be an introvert and a homebody, so this trip and signing has already challenged him. I probably shouldn't have canceled that other room without talking to him first.

Candice goes over the amenities at the resort, as well as where our room is, what we'll find there, and all the dining options. She says we can schedule a time with a resort specialist to book shows, events, and activities, and we promise to do that tomorrow.

By the time we get our key and Candice clicks away in her professional heels, I've drunk my entire fruity cocktail, and Logan looks like he could easily down two. He hasn't taken a single taste of his, and I nudge it toward him.

He picks it up and takes a sip. "You planned this, didn't you?"

I wish I had a drink to hide behind, but I don't. So I hold his gaze evenly and say, "Why pay for two rooms when we both want to be in the same one?"

His eyes dance with light and life. "Fine. But I get to pick your swimwear each day."

I laugh, tipping my head back and letting the warmth of the alcohol make me a little tipsy. "Deal."

He picks up the folder and stands. "Come on," he says. "Let's go see what the view is like from *our* room."

"Yes," I say, quickly joining him and linking my arm through his. I'm the luckiest woman in the world to be on his arm, and I know it keenly. We've talked about marriage for the better part of a year now, and Logan still hasn't proposed. I'm not anxious for him to do so, but I'd be lying if I said I wasn't hoping he'd packed a ring in his bags.

"Let's go see what the view is like from our room."

The view from our room is indescribable. The floor shines like white gold it's so polished and clean. It has to be marble, but Logan says it's probably not. I don't disagree with him, because I'm swept away by the huge bed in the middle of the room, with its cool, blue comforter and mountains—and I mean *mountains*—of pillows. They're dressed in white cases, and I flop back on the bed in bliss.

"It's like lying on cotton candy," I say.

Logan chuckles as he puts his bag against the wall. "Nice sitting room. She was right about that."

I manage to push myself up and drink in the rest of the room. The walls are gray, with beautiful landscapes of the beach done in watercolors. I like them so much more than photographs, and I watch Logan pick up one of the pillows on the full-sized couch. It looks like it's made of denim, which I love, and the pillows are yellow, blue, and pink. Very calming and serene.

There's a tiny table in the corner with only two chairs, and the heavy, blackout drapes are open, but the gauzy privacy ones aren't.

The Relationtrip

We're on the fifth floor here—the highest one—and Logan turns back to me, his hand on the wand to open the curtains. "Ready?"

I jump up and join him. "Ready." I can already see the sunlight glittering outside. There are no palm trees here like there are in Cayman, Florida, Mexico, or Belize. I can't even believe I'm standing here, in this country, on another continent, with the man I love.

It's all too much.

He opens the curtains, and we both stand very still for a moment. We both breathe in together, but it's me who goes, "Oh, this is better than I even imagined." I fumble to open the slider door, and out we both spill. The balcony spans the width of the room, and there's no hot tub on this one.

There is a breakfast nook, and I wrap my arms around Logan, pleased when he wraps me up too. We gaze out past the blissfully beige sand to the ocean beyond. "It's beautiful," I murmur.

"I love it here," Logan whispers. "We should move to Australia."

I gaze up at him. "We should."

He looks down at me. "You would die without your mom and sisters."

"Die?" I scoff, though he's right. We aren't going to move to Sydney, Australia. If we did, we wouldn't be able to return on our mid-winter trip. "I wouldn't die."

"I don't want to move here," he says, returning his

attention to the beach and the water. "I just want to get married on the beach. Our life in Pittsburgh is what I want. Then we can visit places like this and truly enjoy them."

"On which beach do you want to marry me?"

"You're supposed to pick that." He grins at me and lowers his mouth to touch mine lightly. He kisses me gently, which only makes my blood burn hotter than the mid-winter sun in the Southern hemisphere. He breaks the kiss, but keeps his mouth very close to mine. "Am I copping out if I ask you to marry me right here?"

I yank away from him, my pulse positively racing now. "Logan?"

He drops to both knees right in front of me, his face glowing like the sun bathing us. "Sloane Sanders, my life changed at a ticket counter six years ago. This gorgeous woman took me on her non-honeymoon, and you've been my best friend ever since. I can't wait to build our life together. Will you marry me?"

"Yes," I whisper. He digs in his shorts pocket and lifts up a ring with a gold double-band, the diamond glinting in the Australian light. It's not huge but large enough to catch the light and throw it around the balcony. "Yes, Logan, yes."

I hold my hand out, and he slips the ring onto my finger. He kisses the back of my hand, then turns it over to touch his lips to the inside of my wrist. I lean down and take his face in my hands. "I love you. I can't wait to be your wife."

"I love you too." He rises to his feet, takes me into his arms again, and kisses me like a man who just got engaged.

Because he did.

* * *

Keep reading for a sneak peek at the first book in a beach romcom series - **JUST HIS SECRETARY**. I write these under Donna Jeffries, and they feel a lot like this book - except they're enemies to lovers workplace romances!

Like this book? **Reviews are appreciated and welcome, on any retailer, BookBub, or Goodreads.** They can be as long or as short as you'd like. Even star ratings are wonderful. Thank you!

Sneak Peek! Just His Secretary
Chapter One:

My phone chimes, the sound of a high-pitched, toy car engine. My ride has arrived.

I'm not quite ready to leave, but I did call the ride, and I can't keep putting off this conversation. If my boss wasn't quite so grumpy and if he didn't already pay me quite so well, I wouldn't feel so nervous about asking for a raise.

Honestly, Dawson Tightwad Houser should've *offered* me the raise months ago.

The only reason he hasn't been paying me more all this time is because of my own chickenness in asking him to.

"Today," I mutter to myself, reaching for the cup of pink grapefruit segments. I like to start the day out with the intent of eating well. I'll be sorting Skittles by lunchtime, and I remember that I'm down to my last three bags.

I'll have to find someone to drive me to the warehouse store to get another box. I buy the candy in bulk, the way movie theaters do, because I can save thirty-eight cents per bag over buying them at the corner market I can walk to.

The doorbell rings, and I snatch my purse off the kitchen counter and take it with my grapefruit segments toward the door. "Sorry," I say as I open the door. "I'm coming."

"Callie Michaels?" the man standing there asks. He's wearing a ball cap with the NY on it for the Yankees, a gray T-shirt with the same logo, and a pair of navy blue sweat pants that hang on his skinny frame.

He's a few inches taller than me, even in my cute ankle boots with a three-inch heel, and he's just my type. Aloof, sure, but most guys are when meeting a pretty woman.

I smile at him, hoping I'm pretty enough for the likes of him. "Yep, Callie Michaels."

"I'm Chris." He flashes me a smile in return.

I pull my phone out. "I'm sending my girlfriend the info of my ride in case I disappear."

He chuckles and turns to go down my front steps. I love my little blue house. It sits at the end of a dead-end street, and has one of the biggest live oaks in the neighborhood standing guard in the front yard.

"Tara's already responded," I say, stepping out of the house and pulling my front door closed. As I go down the steps, I run through my mental checklist for leaving the house.

Stove, off. That's important too, as I've left it on before, and all those things my mother used to worry about happening if someone would be such a disaster to leave the stove on when they left the house—those happened.

The candle I'd had beside the stove had melted everywhere. The oozing wax had soaked into the bottom of the roll of paper towels, and it had fallen over.

Onto the hot burner. And then that paper had ignited.

My neighbor had seen the smoke and called the fire department. I'd gotten a call at work about my house burning down, and in a surprise move, my boss had driven me home so I could deal with the situation.

Dawson hadn't even fired me for leaving work early. I'd heard he'd let go of plenty of previous secretaries for less.

"Can I practice my pitch on you?" I ask as I slide into the front passenger seat. "Is it okay if I ride up here? I always feel so lame in the back seat."

"Sure," Chris said. "And pitch away."

"Okay." I smooth down my pencil skirt and settle my bright green briefcase bag near my feet. "Just a sec."

I glance toward the house and find Claude Monet perched in the windowsill, his frowny cat face clearly showing me his opinion of my departure. He likes to watch the birds from that spot, and he'll run outside the moment I arrive home from work tonight.

He has no claws, but he sure does like to pretend he

can climb a tree and catch one of those blue-black birds that like to torment him.

Feed the cat, check.

Took a pound of ground beef out of the freezer so I can make mini-meatloaves for dinner tonight. Ready.

Texted Tara about my ride, done.

Tucked all the folders for the meeting with the big wigs from Veterans Brew, the coffee company that would fund my raise if everything went well this afternoon, into my bag. Yep.

"All right," I say. "First off, I've been in this job for five years. That's about four years and eleven months longer than any other secretary who's worked with my boss." I glance at Chris, and he's nodding.

"Second, I'm really good at my job. My boss texts me at home to find out where his blazer is, for crying out loud."

"Sounds dysfunctional," he says, peering up at the stoplight to make sure it's still red. "Is this the pitch?"

"No, just background," I say. "One more quick point. I have a master's degree in marketing and human resources." I wave my hand and resist the urge to tuck my hair behind my ear.

Dawson once commented that whenever I did that, he knew I was nervous, and he didn't want the men and women we met with to know that too. I work really hard not to do it in front of him anymore.

Just another reason I deserve this raise, I tell myself.

"Okay, here's the pitch." I draw a deep breath, hold it, gather my thoughts, and exhale. "I've been at Dawson Dials In for over five years now. I'm never late, despite not owning a car. The filing system has never been neater. We've increased the business here by four hundred percent since I started here, and your firm had barely been operating in the black when I started. Now, everything runs like a well-oiled machine."

All true. A lot of that has to do with Dawson, sure. He has the degrees and the training and a creative mind like none I've witnessed before.

But he has a strong, smart, organized woman—me— behind the front he puts on for everyone who walks through the door of the marketing firm that employs only the two of us.

"I haven't had a raise in sixteen months, and I think I deserve one." I nod, having reached the end of my pitch. I've practiced it in front of the mirror, wearing my sexiest set of underwear.

Leopard print. *Pink* leopard print.

I wear the same bra and panties now, because they make me feel powerful. They're like a naughty little secret only I know, and that makes me feel a step above Dawson, as if I know something he doesn't.

As if the man cares about what I wear under my clothes. In all the time I've known him, the man has never been on a date. Has never even called a woman, except clients and the landlord we pay rent to.

He isn't a workaholic, because he leaves the office by five p.m. every evening.

He isn't ugly either. In all honesty, he's downright hot. Power suits, shiny shoes, thick, wavy hair. The beard. Mylanta, the beard. He runs, he plays basketball, and at first glance, he could definitely get any woman he wants.

The truth is, Dawson Houser is a complete beast. An ogre. The quintessential office grump.

"That's it?" Chris asks. "That's the pitch?"

"That's it," I say. "My boss loses interest if I talk for more than thirty seconds."

"And you want to keep this job?" Chris looks at me like I'm nuts.

Sometimes I feel nuts.

I peel back the plastic top on my grapefruit cup. "Yes," I say. "It's a good job. I like it. He pays really well."

And the office is in an old, 1700s house in downtown Charleston, where the second-story window has a killer view of the Atlantic Ocean.

"Then why do you need the raise?" Chris finally leaves the stoplights of Sugar Creek behind and hits the highway.

"I haven't had one for sixteen months," I say, annoyance flashing through me. Didn't he listen to the pitch?

"He's going to ask that," Chris says.

"I outlined why I deserve the raise." I don't want to point out that Dawson will never find someone who can do what I can *and* who can put up with him.

"Well, I don't know..." Chris grins at me, but his laid-back, sporty-jock look only irritates me now.

"Okay," I say, reaching for my bag. "I'll work on it some more."

He adjusts the radio, the music set to the pop favorites. I happen to like the newest, poppiest music, but I don't tell Chris that.

I pretend to go over the notes for the meeting that afternoon, but my mind wanders through my pitch.

No, I tell myself as Chris makes the final turn and eases to a stop in front of the house-office.

"Here you go, Callie Michaels," he says, clearly flirting with me.

"Thank you, Chris Potter." I tap to pay him, and his phone *cha-chings* from where he's attached it to the windshield.

"Hey, before you go," he says, and I know what comes next. I actually smile, because he's going to ask me out, and that means I've put all the parts of myself together well enough to make other people believe I have my life together.

They don't know about the house fire. Or the escaped hamsters. The partial nudity in public. Or the Glue Incident.

So.

"Are you seeing anyone?" he asks. "Maybe you'd like to go to dinner with me sometime."

He has nice eyes, the color of the rich, deep earth that my potted plants sit in. At least until I kill them.

"I'm not seeing anyone at the moment," I say. "When is 'sometime,' Mister Potter?"

"I don't know," he says. "I think I have a date with another pretty woman I drove to work yesterday…"

I laugh, because he *is* cute, and why shouldn't I go out with him? He's clearly not a serial killer.

He could be, I think.

That's why you date, I hear in my head, in my mother's voice. *To find out if he's a serial killer or not.*

"No facial piercings?" I ask, searching that handsome face. "Are you a cat-hater? Wait. Do you only own sweats?" I eye the pants, once again noting how skinny he is.

I need a beefier guy to go with my size twelve body. Fine, size fourteen. But it'll be a good dinner date, and I won't have to eat meatloaf for the third or fourth night in a row.

He swipes on his phone for a moment, his chuckle still filling the car. "Looks like I have to work tomorrow, and my mom is going to do our monthly *are-you-dating-anyone* dinner on Wednesday…Thursday?"

He looks up, hopeful.

"Sure," I say. "Thursday."

"I'll text you right now, and then you'll have my number."

"Perfect." I've already tucked my phone away, because

Dawson doesn't like it when I walk in, glued to my phone. I feel the device vibrate against my foot, and I add, "I got it. Now, wish me luck with my raise."

"Good luck with your raise," he says dutifully, and I giggle again as I get out of the car.

Facing the house, though, I erase all signs of joviality. It's time for work, and that means I need my best game face securely in place.

"You've got this," I whisper to myself as I walk down the sidewalk. "You're smart. You're capable. You've taken this company from floundering to thriving. You, Callie. It's Monday morning, and you have meetings with this man specifically to talk about this kind of thing."

I put my hand on the door handle and take another breath. I'm going to slay this Monday.

I open the door, my cute bag on my shoulder and my leopard underwear concealed beneath adorable, professional attire.

This raise is mine, I think...at least until I hear Dawson yell, "It better be here by ten, or someone's going to lose their head!"

Sneak Peek! Just His Secretary
Chapter Two:

I cannot believe the guy on the other end of the line. "This is unacceptable," I say next, taking my bellow down to a mere yell. It might even simply be how I'd call out to Callie, my secretary.

She appears in the doorway, her perfectly sculpted eyebrows raised toward the ceiling. I wave her inside as the guy explains to me about an accident his bike courier experienced that morning.

"Then get another courier," I say. "And if those renditions are damaged at all, I swear, I'll make sure no one uses your services again."

Callie enters the office, her tartly green-apple bag hanging from her forearm. She strides in, which I like. She's not afraid of me, even when I'm on the edge of rage.

She's dressed perfectly for this afternoon's meeting, though she wears a skirt five days a week. I'd told her she could dress down on Fridays, but I never do, and I guess she picked up on my cues.

Today, her blouse reminds me of a field of flowers, and the CEO of Veterans Brew loves poppies.

She's got those, and some violet blooms, as well as some flower that's yellow. The greenery flowing over the white, silky fabric makes her the epitome of spring, and I'm male enough to notice her curves.

"Fine," I bark into the phone as the owner of the courier company tells me he'll drive over the renditions of the marketing materials we need for that afternoon himself. "By ten o'clock."

I slam the phone down and run both hands through my hair. "Good morning," I say with a sigh.

"Is it?" Callie asks.

When I look at her, she tilts her head, her expression open and questioning at the same time.

"No," I say. "The bike courier got in an accident this morning, and the renditions of the posters won't be here until ten."

"Should we postpone the morning meeting until we get them?" She bends to open her bag, taking out several folders and putting them on the edge of my desk.

I'm tired already, and it's Monday morning. I suppress a sigh and run my fingers down my beard instead. I reach for the glasses I need to see things close up, though I haven't told anyone that they should be a permanent feature on my face. Callie thinks they're reading glasses, and since I'll be reading her notes, I'm fine to wear them.

"No," I say. "Let's go over the week." I reach for the notes she's extracted, but she doesn't extend them toward me.

I lift my eyes to hers, and if I still dated women—which I don't—I'd be looking for a pair of eyes the color of hers. Bright blue, like a perfect summery sky over South Carolina. The kind I experienced as a kid, sitting on the beach at the fancy resort my parents had taken me to.

I swallow, something sparking inside me that had died the day Kim had left me standing at the altar.

"What's going on?" I growl, a third at her for refusing to give me the notes, a third for the late renditions, and a third at the stupid way my hormones and body have reacted to my secretary.

I've told more people than I can count that she's just my secretary. So many clients and customers have commented on how well we work together and how cute we are as a couple.

"She's just my secretary," has come out of my mouth dozens of times, almost like a parrot.

She's said it too, and she's never once indicated that she'd like to spend any more time with me than she has to.

"I'd like to speak with you about something first," she says, reaching up and tucking her long, sandy-blonde hair behind her ear.

She's nervous.

I lean back in my chair, suddenly nervous too. "You're quitting."

"What?" She shakes her head. "No." A light, girlish giggle comes from her mouth, and I glare at her.

She silences it. She's a couple of years younger than me, and some men like giggling. I am not one of them. I barely tolerate the stuffed animals she brings into the office for Valentine's Day, and the fruity candles she's forever lighting to make the office smell more homey drive me to the brink of madness.

Most things do, in all honesty. Including the way my stupid male side wonders what her very female mouth would taste like.

My hormones rear up every few months, and I have to tamp them back down into the box where I keep them. Sometimes I'll chat with someone via a dating app or even go to dinner with Lance, my best friend, and his girlfriend. That reminds me how much I do *not* want to be tied down, and I'm good for a while.

"I want a raise," Callie blurts out. Her eyes widen, and she shakes her shoulders slightly. "I mean, I've been here for over five years now, Mister Houser. You were barely operating in the black then, and now this place is turning customers away."

She has a ton to do with that, and I'm not oblivious to that fact.

"It's been sixteen months since my last raise, and I believe I'm due."

I steeple my fingers in front of my face and consider her request.

She nods, her pitch done. I do like that about her. I have a list of things I'd like to discuss for this week too, and we need to go over our afternoon meeting.

"Fine," I say again, this time with much less animosity in my voice. "Another twelve?"

"That would be wonderful," she says, her smile professional though her eyes now dance with merriment.

I can admit I'm glad she's happy. The rope that is always wound tight inside me releases a little bit. "Now, can we go over the notes?"

"Yes, sir," she says, handing them to me. "We also need to discuss a possible new cleaner, as you mentioned it last week. And I'd like to change the fresh flower delivery to bi-weekly instead of weekly."

"I have a list too." I take the notes from her and hand her the list I've scrawled on a scrap of paper from a pad my mother gave me for Christmas last year.

She takes that and we study what we've been given. "Your mother is coming Thursday?" she asks, plenty of surprise in her voice.

I look up and find her frowning. "Yes," I say. "I just found out."

"You better have," she said, exchanging my list for her phone. "You do know how hard it is to get a housekeeper on such short notice, right?" She lifts her phone to her ear. "You do need me to get someone to clean your house, yes?"

"Yes, please," I say, embarrassed my secretary has to do such a thing for me.

She sighs and looks at my list again. "It's a good thing I've got my power panties on today," she says. "Or I'd never get all of this done."

I choke, not used to talking about unmentionables across my desk. At least not with Callie.

Not with anyone, I remind myself.

"Your what?"

Callie gasps and claps one hand over her mouth, her eyes wide as dinner plates and stuck on mine.

The moment between us is almost funny, if I wasn't now thinking about what she has on beneath her clothes.

She jerks to attention a moment later and says in an ultra-crisp voice, "Yes, hi, I know it's last-minute, but I need someone to clean an eighteen-hundred square-foot house before Thursday morning."

Grab **Just His Secretary** in paperback or ebook by scanning the code below with your phone.

The Relationtrip

Books in the Southern Roots Sweet RomCom Series

Just His Secretary, Book 1: She's just his secretary...until he needs someone on his arm to convince his mother that he can take over the family business. Then Callie becomes Dawson's girlfriend—but just in his text messages...but maybe she'll start to worm her way into his shriveled heart too.

Just His Boss, Book 2: She's just his boss, especially since Tara just barely hired Alec. But when things heat up in the kitchen, Tara will have to decide where Alec is needed more —on her arm or behind the stove.

Just His Assistant, Book 3: She's just his assistant, which is exactly how this Southern belle wants it. No spotlight. Not anymore. But as she struggles to learn her new role in his office—especially because Lance is the surliest boss imaginable—Jessie might just have to open her heart to show him everyone has a past they're running from.

Just His Partner, Book 4: She's just his partner, because she's seen the number of women he parades through his life. No amount of charm and good looks is worth being played...until Sabra witnesses Jason take the blame for someone else at the law office where they both work.

* * *

Just His Barista, Book 5: She's just his barista...until she buys into Legacy Brew as a co-owner. Then she's Coy's business partner *and* the source of his five-year-long crush. But after they share a kiss one night, Macie's seriously considering mixing business and pleasure.

Books in the Hilton Head Romance series

The Love List (Hilton Head Romance, Book 1): Bea turns to her lists when things get confusing and her love list morphs once again... Can she add *fall in love at age 45* to the list and check it off?

The Paradise Plan (Hilton Head Romance, Book 2): When Harrison keeps showing up unannounced at her construction site, sometimes with her favorite pastries, Cass starts to wonder if she should add him to her daily routine... If she does, will her perfectly laid out plans fall short of paradise? Or could she find her new life *and* a new love, all without any plans at all?

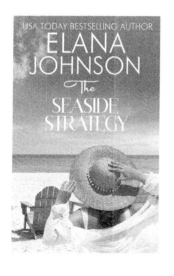

The Seaside Strategy (Hilton Head Romance, Book 3): Lauren doesn't want to work for Blake, especially not in strategic investments. She's had enough of the high-profile, corporate life. **Can she strategically insert herself into Blake's life without compromising her seaside strategy and finally get what she really wants...love and a lasting relationship?**

The Beach Blueprint (Hilton Head Romance, Book 4): Joy Bartlett needs a blueprint before she takes a single step in any direction. She loves seeing what she's getting into before committing, and moving 1200 miles from Texas to South Carolina just because half of her Supper Club has doesn't mean she's going to start packing boxes. Can she figure out how to arrange all of the pieces in her life in a way that makes sense? Or will she find herself cut off from everyone who's ever been important to her?

Books in the Getaway Bay Romance series

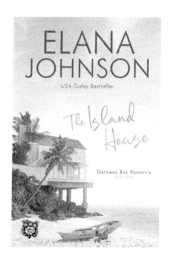

The Island House (Book 1): Charlotte Madsen's whole world came crashing down six months ago with the words, "I met someone else."

Can Charlotte navigate the healing process to find love again?

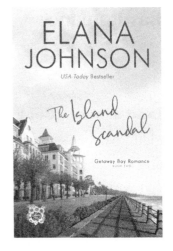

The Island Scandal (Book 2): Ashley Fox has known three things since age twelve: she was an excellent seamstress, what her wedding would look like, and that she'd never leave the island of Getaway Bay. Now, at age 35, she's been right about two of them, at least.

Can Burke and Ash find a way to navigate a romance when they've only ever been friends?

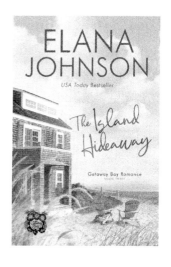

The Island Hideaway (Book 3): She's 37, single (except for the cat), and a synchronized swimmer looking to make some extra cash. Pathetic, right? She thinks so, and she's going to spend this summer housesitting a cliffside hideaway and coming up with a plan to turn her life around.

Can Noah and Zara fight their feelings for each other as easily as they trade jabs? Or will this summer shape up to be the one that provides the romance they've each always wanted?

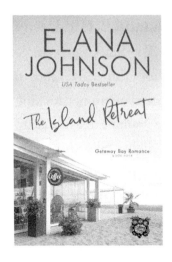

The Island Retreat (Book 4): Shannon's 35, divorced, and the highlight of her day is getting to the coffee shop before the morning rush. She tells herself that's fine, because she's got two cats and a past filled with emotional abuse. But she might be ready to heal so she can retreat into the arms of a man she's known for years...

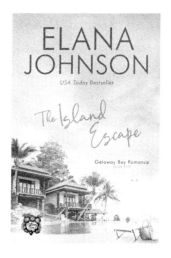

The Island Escape (Book 5): Riley Randall has spent eight years smiling at new brides, being excited for her friends as they find Mr. Right, and dating by a strict set of rules that she never breaks. But she might have to consider bending those rules ever so slightly if she wants an escape from the island...

The Island Storm (Book 6): Lisa is 36, tired of the dating scene in Getaway Bay, and practically the only wedding planner at her company that hasn't found her own happy-ever-after. She's tried dating apps and blind dates...but could the company party put a man she's known for years into the spotlight?

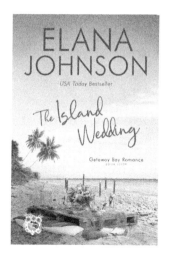

The Island Wedding (Book 7): Deirdre is almost 40, estranged from her teenaged daughter, and determined not to feel sorry for herself. She does the best she can with the cards life has dealt her and she's dreaming of another island wedding...but it certainly can't happen with the widowed Chief of Police.

Books in the Sweet Water Falls Farm Romance series

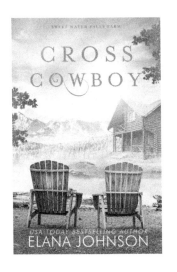

Cross Cowboy, Book 1: He's been accused of being far too blunt. Like that time he accused her of stealing her company from her best friend... Can Travis and Shayla overcome their differences and find a happily-ever-after together?

Grumpy Cowboy

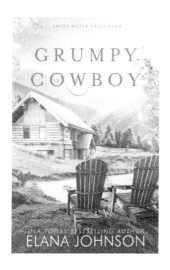

Grumpy Cowboy, Book 2: He can find the negative in any situation. Like that time he got upset with the woman who brought him a free chocolate-and-caramel-covered apple because it had melted in his truck... Can William and Gretchen start over and make a healthy relationship after it's started to wilt?

Surly Cowboy

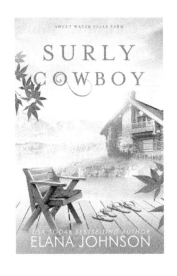

Surly Cowboy, Book 3: He's got a reputation to uphold and he's not all that amused the way regular people are. Like that time he stood there straight-faced and silent while everyone else in the audience cheered and clapped for that educational demo... Can Lee and Rosalie let bygones be bygones and make a family filled with joy?

Salty Cowboy

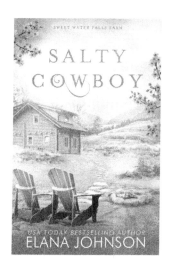

Salty Cowboy, Book 4: The last Cooper sibling is looking for love...she just wishes it wouldn't be in her hometown, or with the saltiest cowboy on the planet. But something about Jed Forrester has Cherry all a-flutter, and he'll be darned if he's going to let her get away. But Jed may have met his match when it comes to his quick tongue and salty attitude...

Books in the Hawthorne Harbor Romance series

The Day He Drove By, Book 1: A widowed florist, her ten-year-old daughter, and the paramedic who delivered the girl a decade earlier...

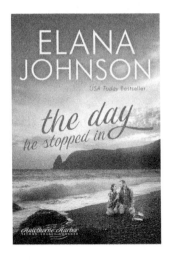

The Day He Stopped In, Book 2: Janey Germaine is tired of entertaining tourists in Olympic National Park all day and trying to keep her twelve-year-old son occupied at night. When longtime friend and the Chief of Police, Adam Herrin, offers to take the boy on a ride-along one fall evening, Janey starts to see him in a different light. Do they have the courage to take their relationship out of the friend zone?

The Day He Said Hello, Book 3: Bennett Patterson is content with his boring fire-fighting job and his big great dane...until he comes face-to-face with his high school girl-friend, Jennie Zimmerman, who swore she'd never return to Hawthorne Harbor. Can they rekindle their old flame? Or will their opposite personalities keep them apart?

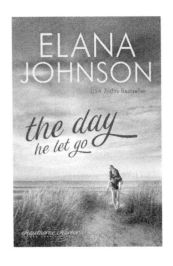

The Day He Let Go, Book 4: Trent Baker is ready for another relationship, and he's hopeful he can find someone who wants him and to be a mother to his son. Lauren Michaels runs her own general contract company, and she's never thought she has a maternal bone in her body. But when she gets a second chance with the handsome K9 cop who blew her off when she first came to town, she can't say no... Can Trent and Lauren make their differences into strengths and build a family?

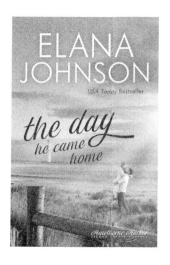

The Day He Came Home, Book 5: A wounded Marine returns to Hawthorne Harbor years after the woman he was married to for exactly one week before she got an annulment...and then a baby nine months later. Can Hunter and Alice make a family out of past heartache?

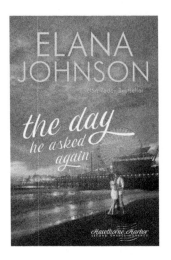

The Day He Asked Again, Book 6: A Coast Guard captain would rather spend his time on the sea...unless he's with the woman he's been crushing on for months. Can Brooklynn and Dave make their second chance stick?

About Elana

Elana Johnson is the USA Today bestselling and Kindle All-Star author of dozens of clean and wholesome contemporary romance novels. She lives in Utah, where she mothers two fur babies, works with her husband full-time, and eats a lot of veggies while writing. Find her on her website at feelgoodfictionbooks.com

Printed in Great Britain
by Amazon

44508169R00192